HARVEY BEAKS™

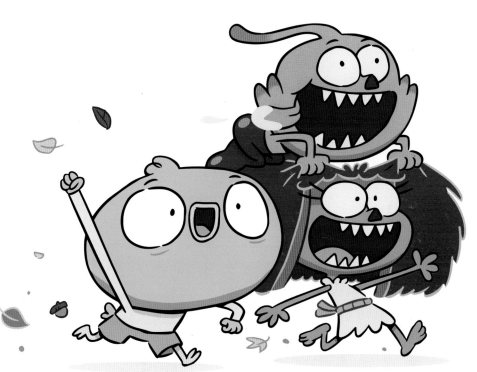

PAPERCUTZ™
NEW YORK

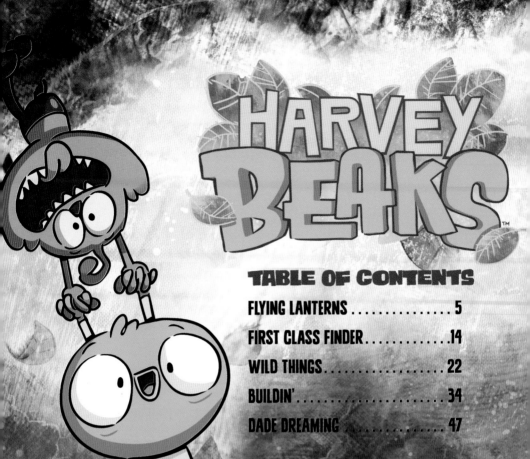

HARVEY BEAKS

TABLE OF CONTENTS

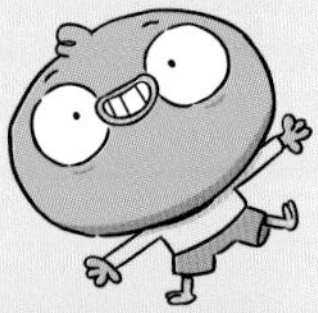

HARVEY BEAKS

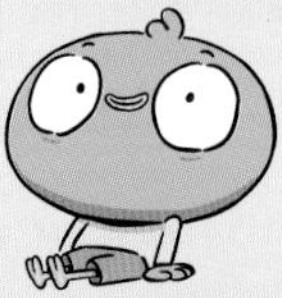

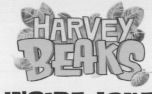

INSIDE JOKE

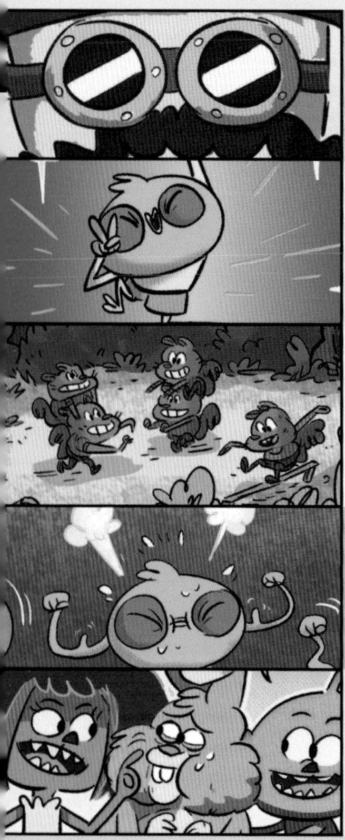

"FLYING LANTERNS"
STEFAN PETRUCHA AND
THE HARVEY BEAKS SHOW WRITERS - WRITERS
ANDREAS SCHUSTER - ARTIST, LETTERER, AND COLORIST

"FIRST CLASS FINDER"
STEFAN PETRUCHA AND
THE HARVEY BEAKS SHOW WRITERS - WRITERS
ANDREAS SCHUSTER - ARTIST & LETTERER
LAURIE E. SMITH - COLORIST

"WILD THINGS"
STEFAN PETRUCHA- WRITER
ANDREAS SCHUSTER - ARTIST & LETTERER
LAURIE E. SMITH - COLORIST

"BUILDIN'"
CARSON MONTGOMERY - WRITER
ANDREAS SCHUSTER - ARTIST & LETTERER
LAURIE E. SMITH - COLORIST

"DADE DREAMING"
SHANE HOUGHTON, WRITER
ANDREAS SCHUSTER - ARTIST & LETTERER
MATT HERMS - COLORIST

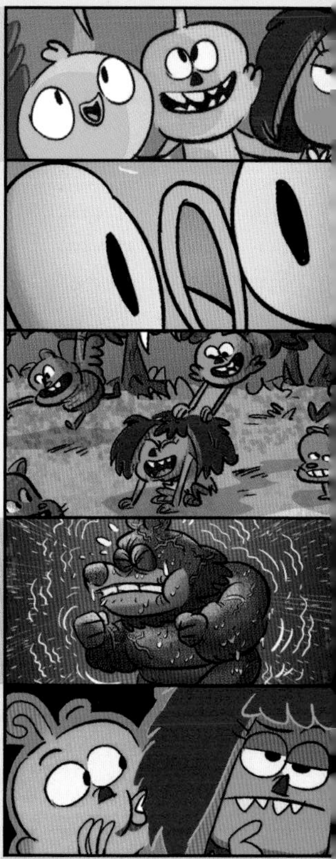

BASED ON THE NICKELODEON ANIMATED TV SERIES CREATED BY C.H. GREENBLATT

JAMES SALERNO - SR. ART DIRECTOR/NICKELODEON
CHRIS NELSON - DESIGN/PRODUCTION
JEFF WHITMAN - PRODUCTION COORDINATOR
BETHANY BRYAN - EDITOR
JOAN HILTY - COMICS EDITOR/NICKELODEON
ASANTE SIMONS - EDITORIAL INTERN
JIM SALICRUP
EDITOR-IN-CHIEF

ISBN: 978-1-62991-431-2 PAPERBACK EDITION
ISBN: 978-1-62991-432-9 HARDCOVER EDITION

PAPERCUTZ BOOKS MAY BE PURCHASED FOR BUSINESS OR PROMOTIONAL USE. FOR INFORMATION ON BULK PURCHASES PLEASE CONTACT MACMILLAN CORPORATE AND PREMIUM SALES DEPARTMENT AT (800) 221-7945 X5442.

PRINTED IN CHINA FEBRUARY 2016 BY IMAGO
2/F, BLK, 402, CAI DIAN INDUSTRIAL ZONE
HUANGGANG NORTH ROAD
FUTIAN DISTRICT, SHENZHEN
CHINA

DISTRIBUTED BY MACMILLAN
FIRST PRINTING

FLYING LANTERNS

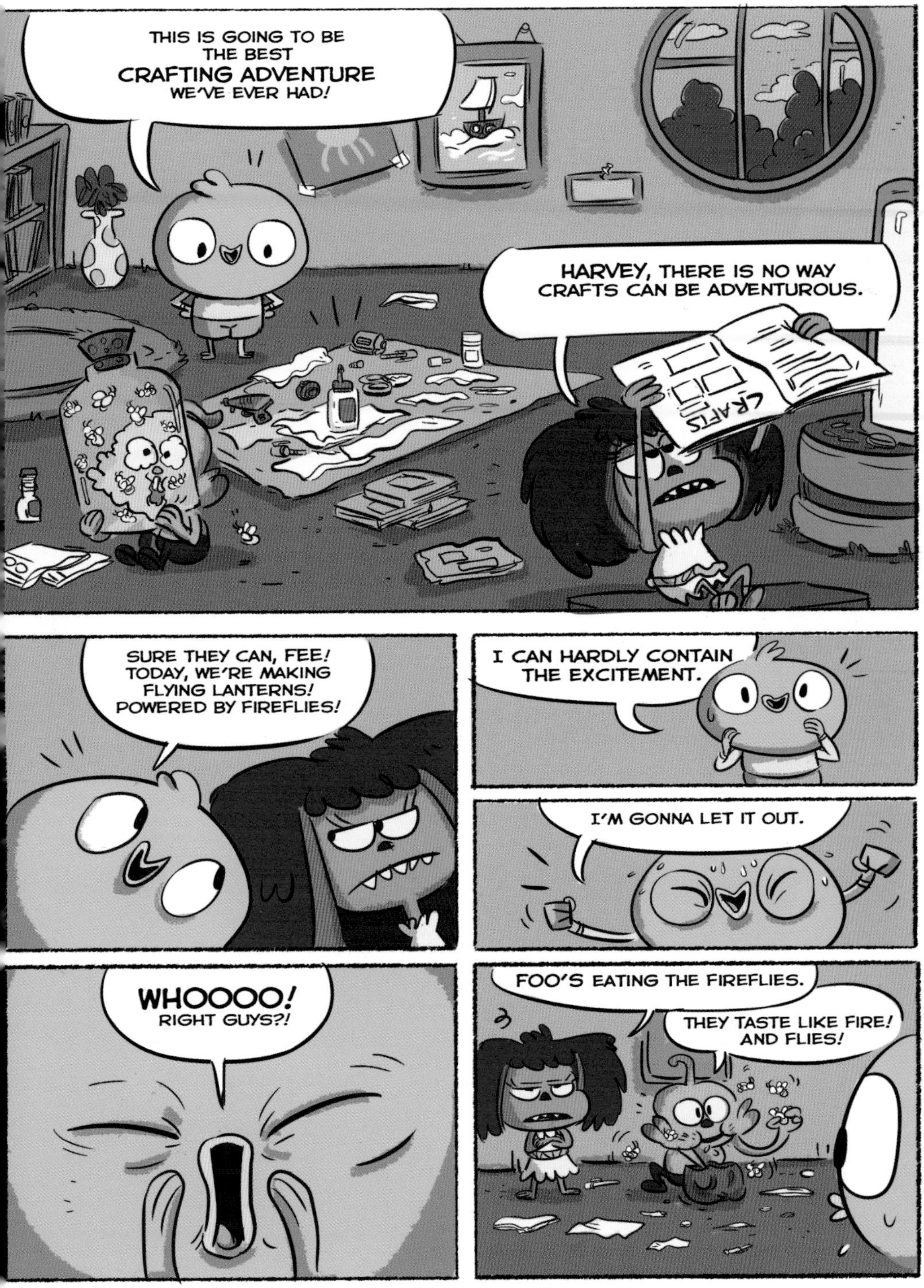
THIS IS GOING TO BE THE BEST CRAFTING ADVENTURE WE'VE EVER HAD!
HARVEY, THERE IS NO WAY CRAFTS CAN BE ADVENTUROUS.
CRAFTS
SURE THEY CAN, FEE! TODAY, WE'RE MAKING FLYING LANTERNS! POWERED BY FIREFLIES!
I CAN HARDLY CONTAIN THE EXCITEMENT.
I'M GONNA LET IT OUT.
WHOOOO! RIGHT GUYS?!
FOO'S EATING THE FIREFLIES.
THEY TASTE LIKE FIRE! AND FLIES!

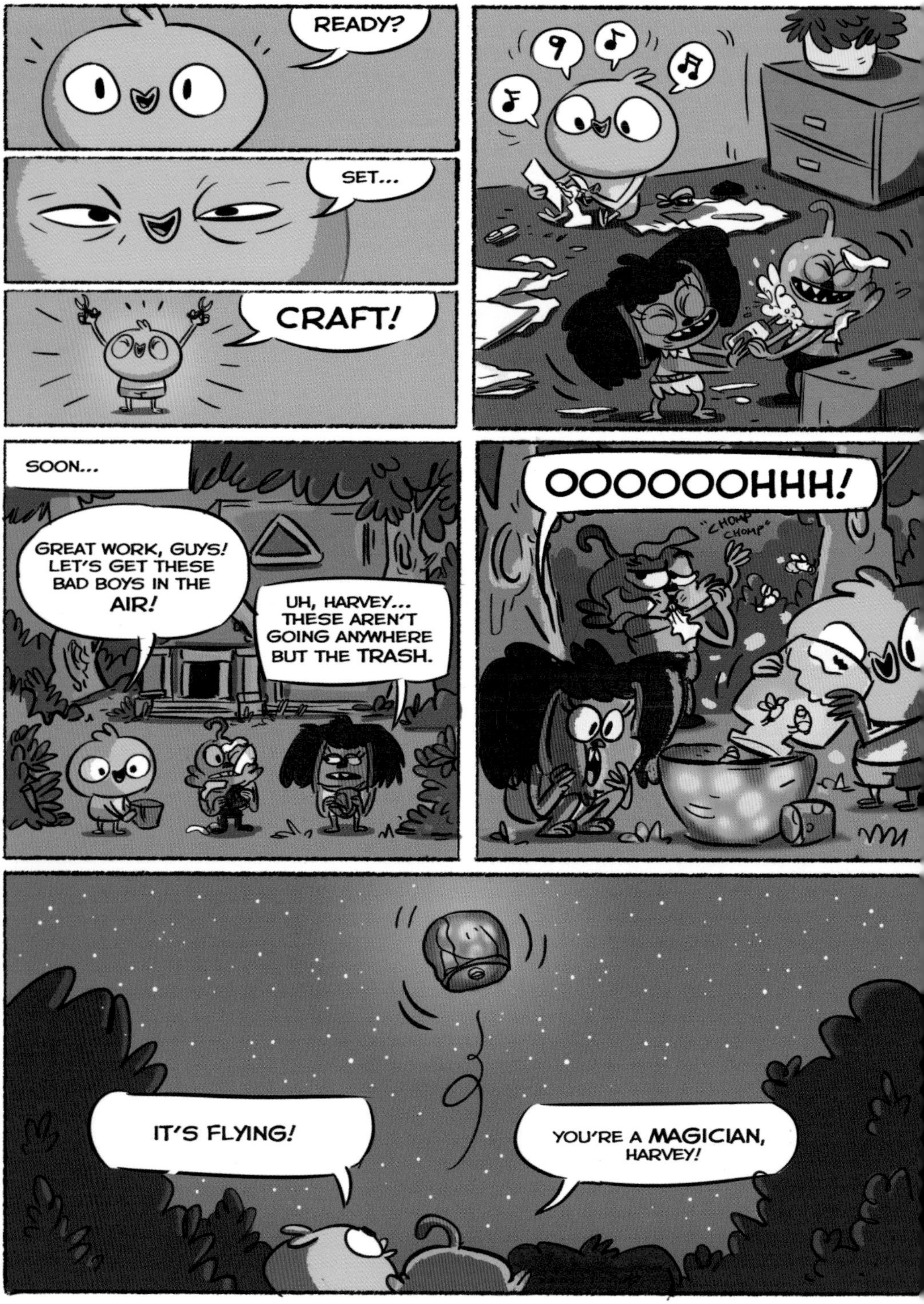
READY?
SET...
CRAFT!
SOON...
GREAT WORK, GUYS! LET'S GET THESE BAD BOYS IN THE AIR!
UH, HARVEY... THESE AREN'T GOING ANYWHERE BUT THE TRASH.
OOOOOOHHH!
CHOMP CHOMP
IT'S FLYING!
YOU'RE A MAGICIAN, HARVEY!

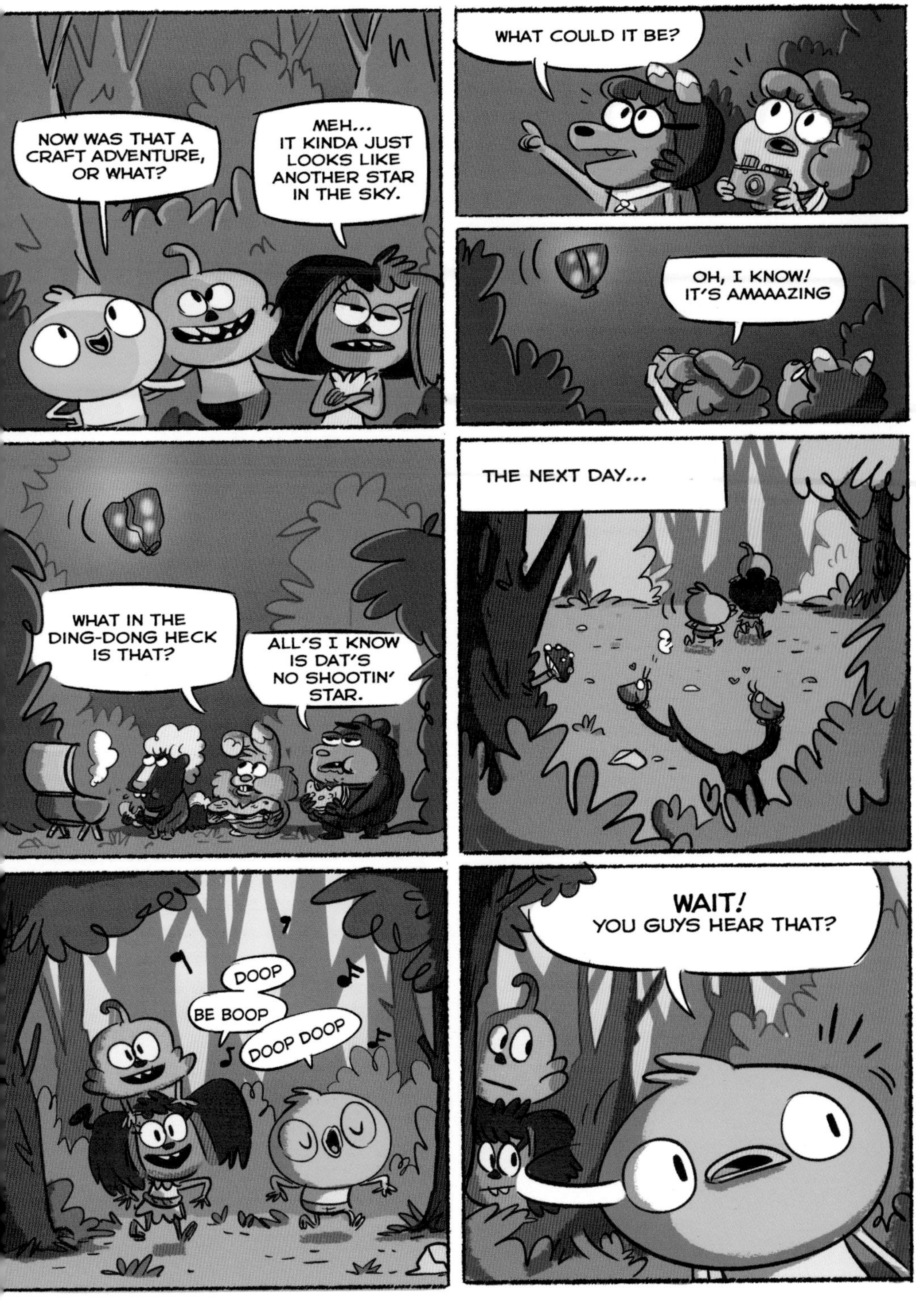
NOW WAS THAT A CRAFT ADVENTURE, OR WHAT?
MEH... IT KINDA JUST LOOKS LIKE ANOTHER STAR IN THE SKY.
WHAT COULD IT BE?
OH, I KNOW! IT'S AMAAAZING
WHAT IN THE DING-DONG HECK IS THAT?
ALL'S I KNOW IS DAT'S NO SHOOTIN' STAR.
THE NEXT DAY...
DOOP
BE BOOP
DOOP DOOP
WAIT! YOU GUYS HEAR THAT?

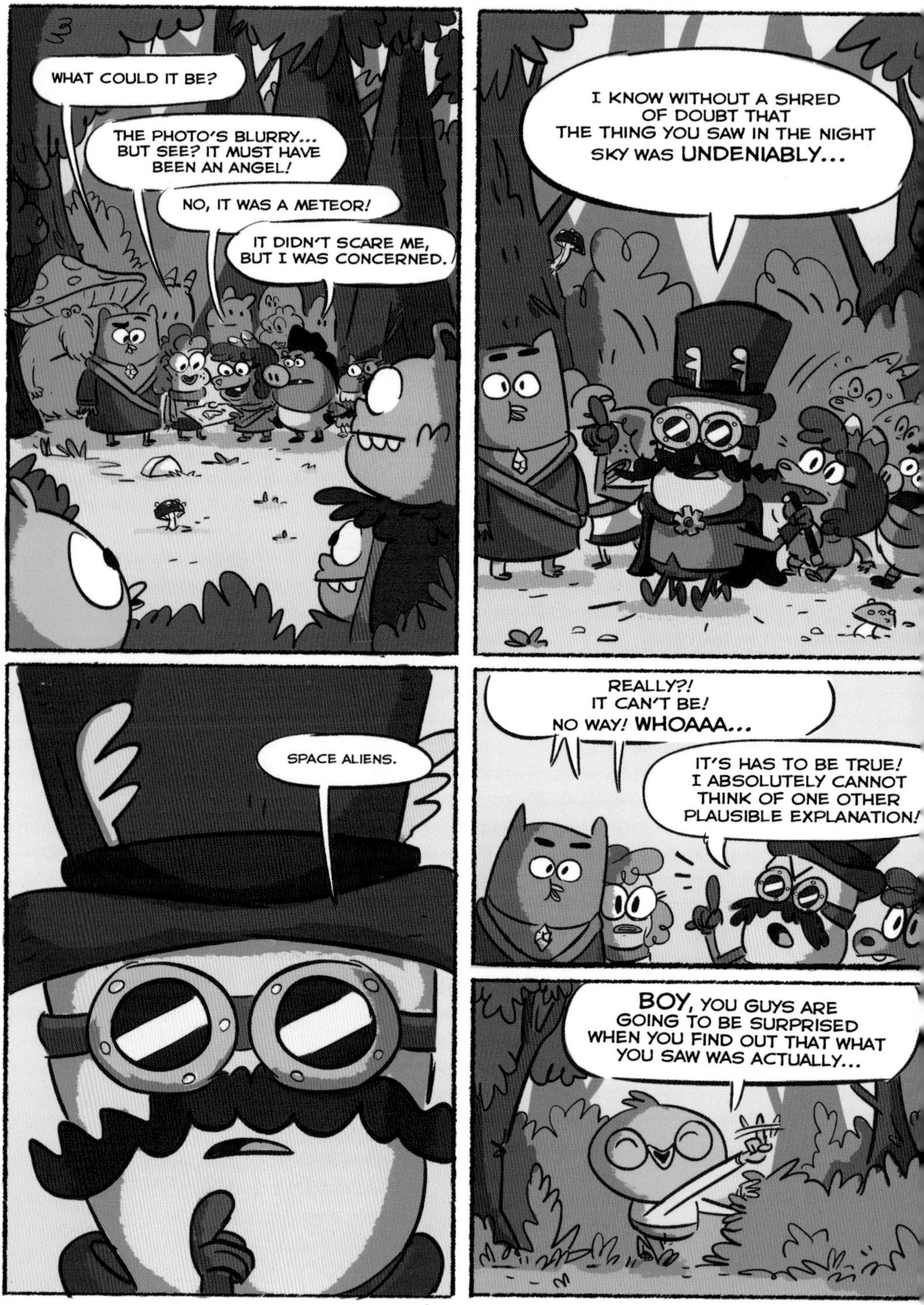
WHAT COULD IT BE?
THE PHOTO'S BLURRY... BUT SEE? IT MUST HAVE BEEN AN ANGEL!
NO, IT WAS A METEOR!
IT DIDN'T SCARE ME, BUT I WAS CONCERNED.
I KNOW WITHOUT A SHRED OF DOUBT THAT THE THING YOU SAW IN THE NIGHT SKY WAS UNDENIABLY...
SPACE ALIENS.
REALLY?! IT CAN'T BE! NO WAY! WHOAAA...
IT'S HAS TO BE TRUE! I ABSOLUTELY CANNOT THINK OF ONE OTHER PLAUSIBLE EXPLANATION!
BOY, YOU GUYS ARE GOING TO BE SURPRISED WHEN YOU FIND OUT THAT WHAT YOU SAW WAS ACTUALLY...

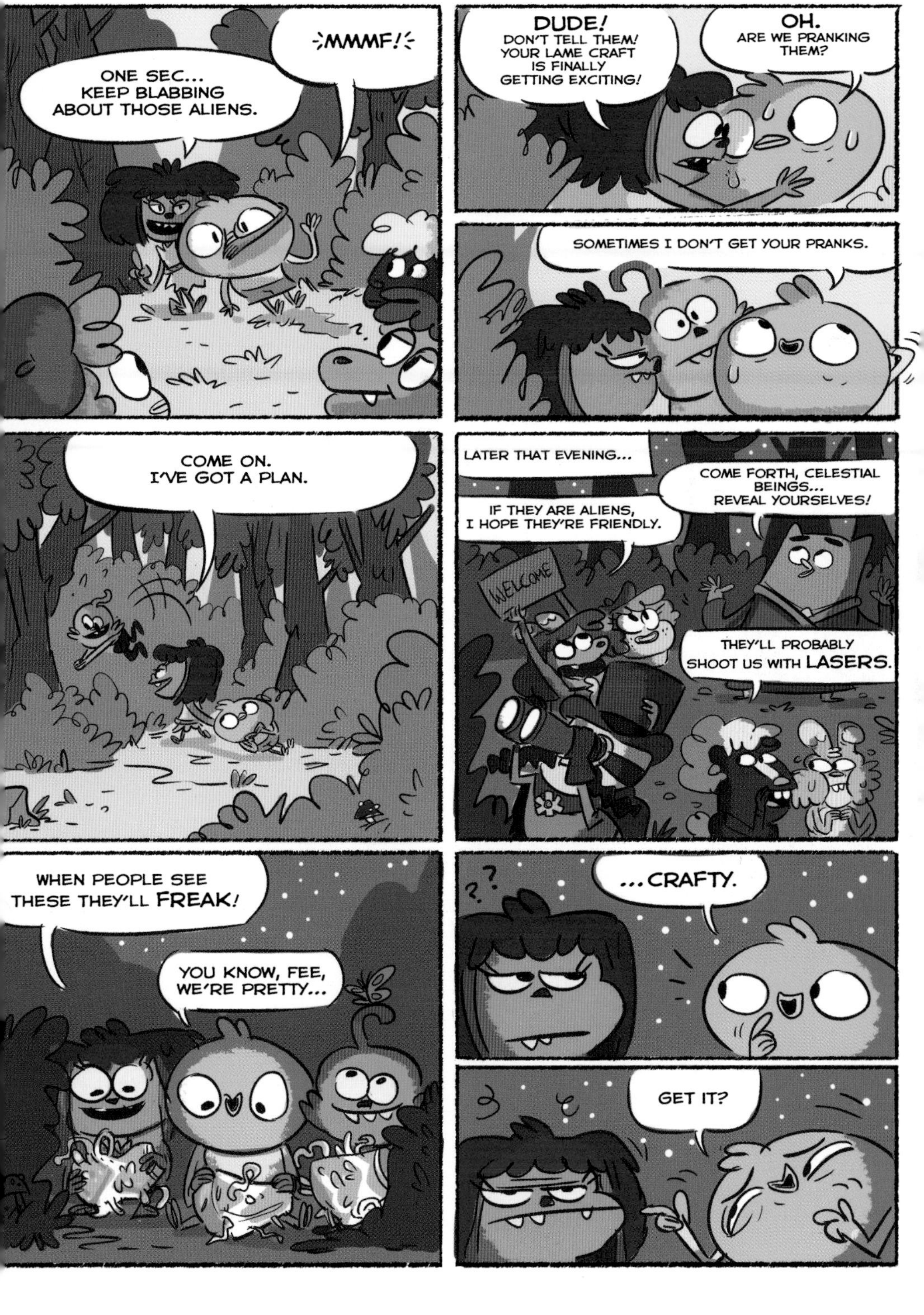

ONE SEC... KEEP BLABBING ABOUT THOSE ALIENS.
MMMF!
DUDE! DON'T TELL THEM! YOUR LAME CRAFT IS FINALLY GETTING EXCITING!
OH. ARE WE PRANKING THEM?
SOMETIMES I DON'T GET YOUR PRANKS.
COME ON. I'VE GOT A PLAN.
LATER THAT EVENING...
COME FORTH, CELESTIAL BEINGS... REVEAL YOURSELVES!
IF THEY ARE ALIENS, I HOPE THEY'RE FRIENDLY.
WELCOME
THEY'LL PROBABLY SHOOT US WITH LASERS.
WHEN PEOPLE SEE THESE THEY'LL FREAK!
YOU KNOW, FEE, WE'RE PRETTY...
??
...CRAFTY.
GET IT?

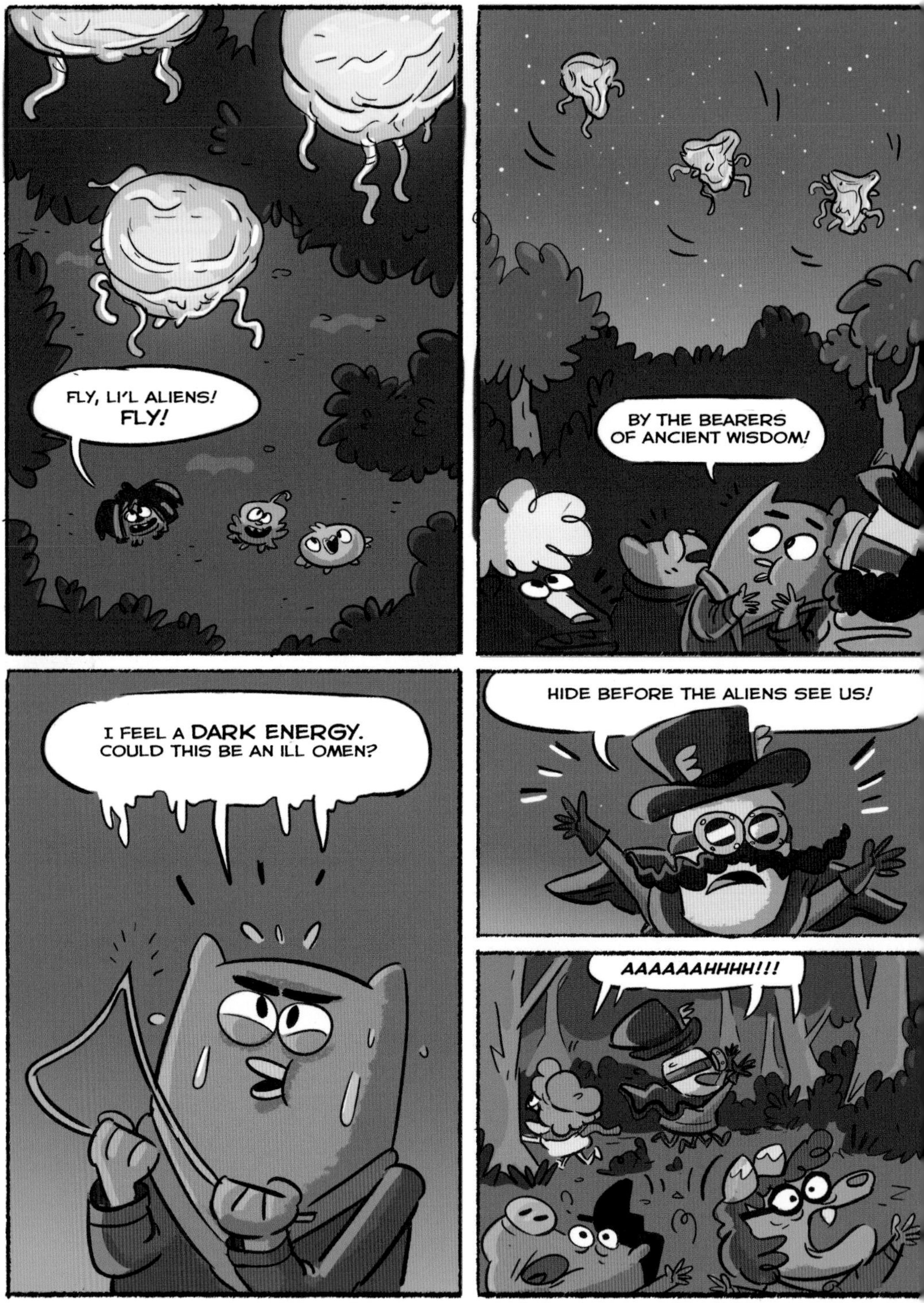
FLY, LI'L ALIENS! FLY!
BY THE BEARERS OF ANCIENT WISDOM!
I FEEL A DARK ENERGY. COULD THIS BE AN ILL OMEN?
HIDE BEFORE THE ALIENS SEE US!
AAAAAAHHHH!!!

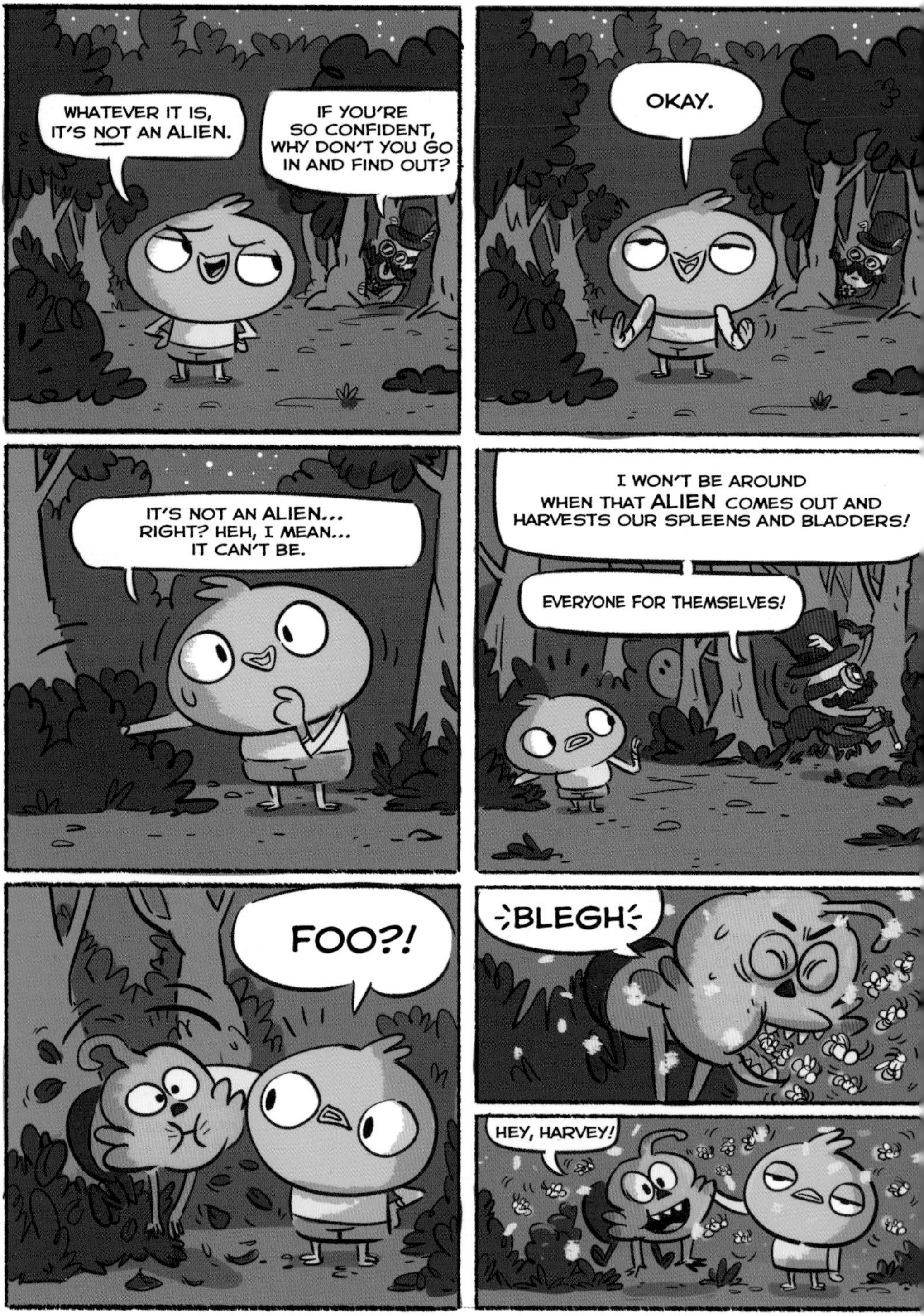
WHATEVER IT IS, IT'S NOT AN ALIEN.
IF YOU'RE SO CONFIDENT, WHY DON'T YOU GO IN AND FIND OUT?
OKAY.
IT'S NOT AN ALIEN... RIGHT? HEH, I MEAN... IT CAN'T BE.
I WON'T BE AROUND WHEN THAT ALIEN COMES OUT AND HARVESTS OUR SPLEENS AND BLADDERS!
EVERYONE FOR THEMSELVES!
FOO?!
BLEGH
HEY, HARVEY!

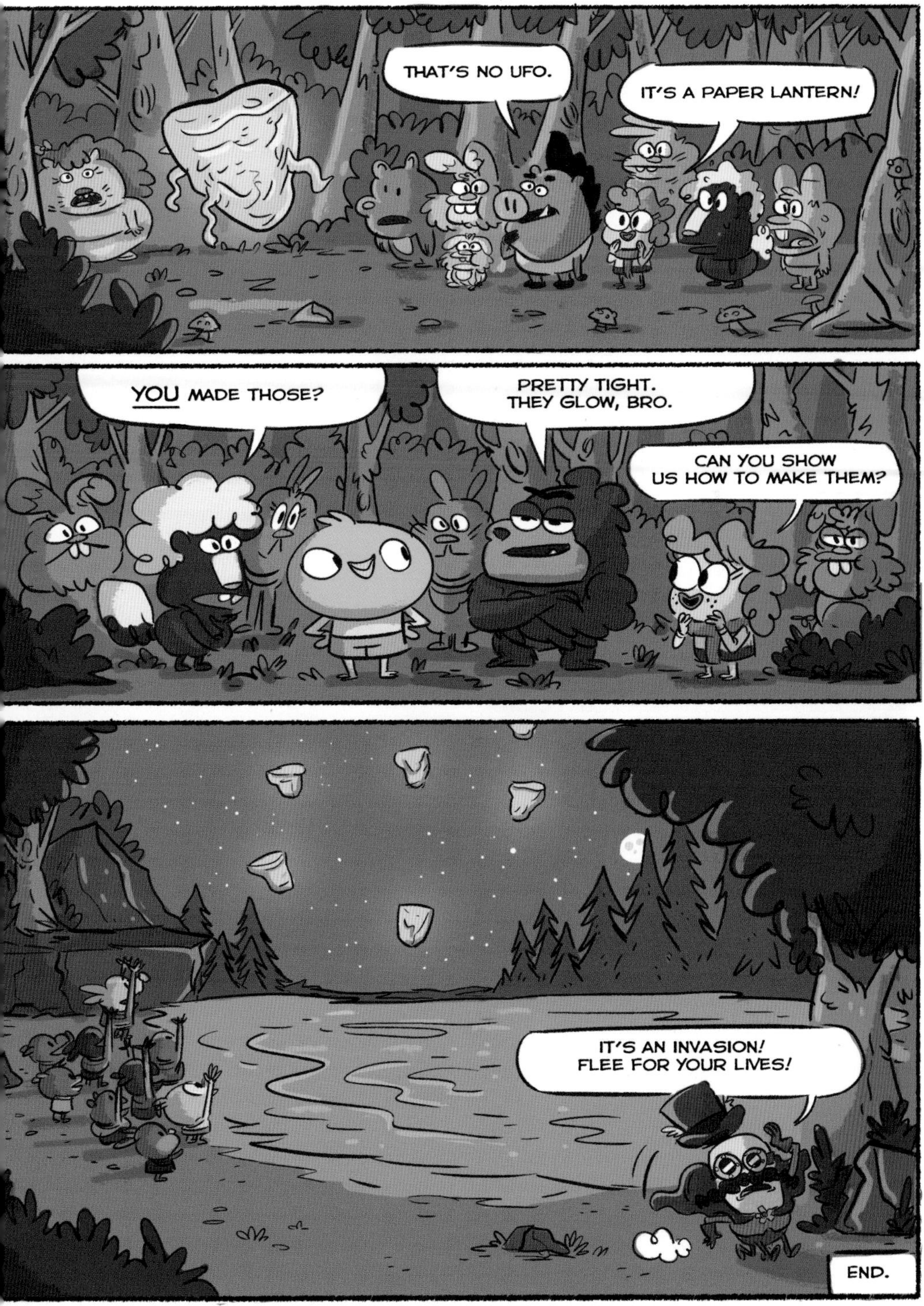
THAT'S NO UFO.
IT'S A PAPER LANTERN!
YOU MADE THOSE?
PRETTY TIGHT. THEY GLOW, BRO.
CAN YOU SHOW US HOW TO MAKE THEM?
IT'S AN INVASION! FLEE FOR YOUR LIVES!
END.

HARVEY BEAKS

FIRST CLASS FINDER

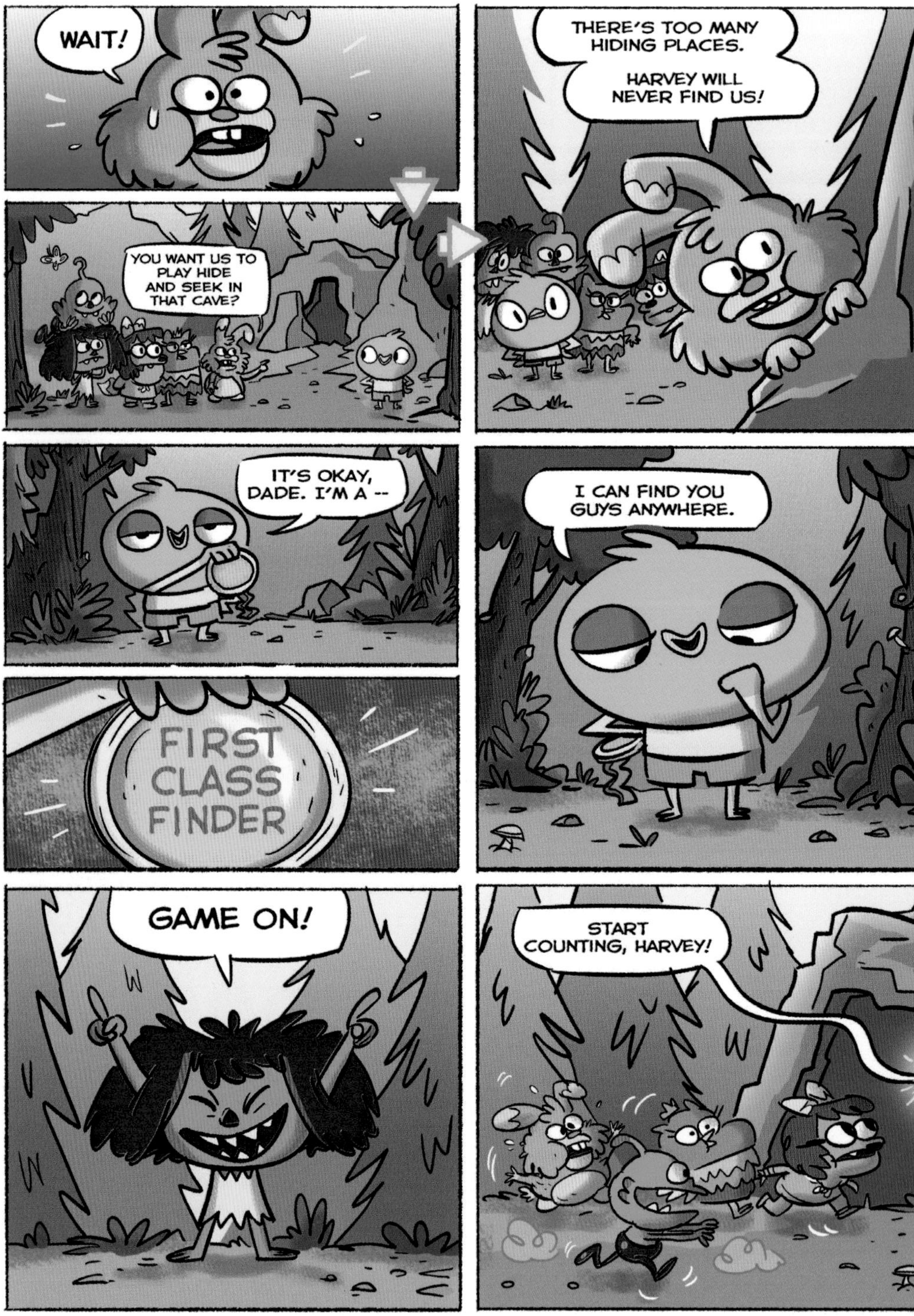
WAIT!
YOU WANT US TO PLAY HIDE AND SEEK IN THAT CAVE?
THERE'S TOO MANY HIDING PLACES.
HARVEY WILL NEVER FIND US!
IT'S OKAY, DADE. I'M A --
FIRST CLASS FINDER
I CAN FIND YOU GUYS ANYWHERE.
GAME ON!
START COUNTING, HARVEY!

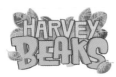

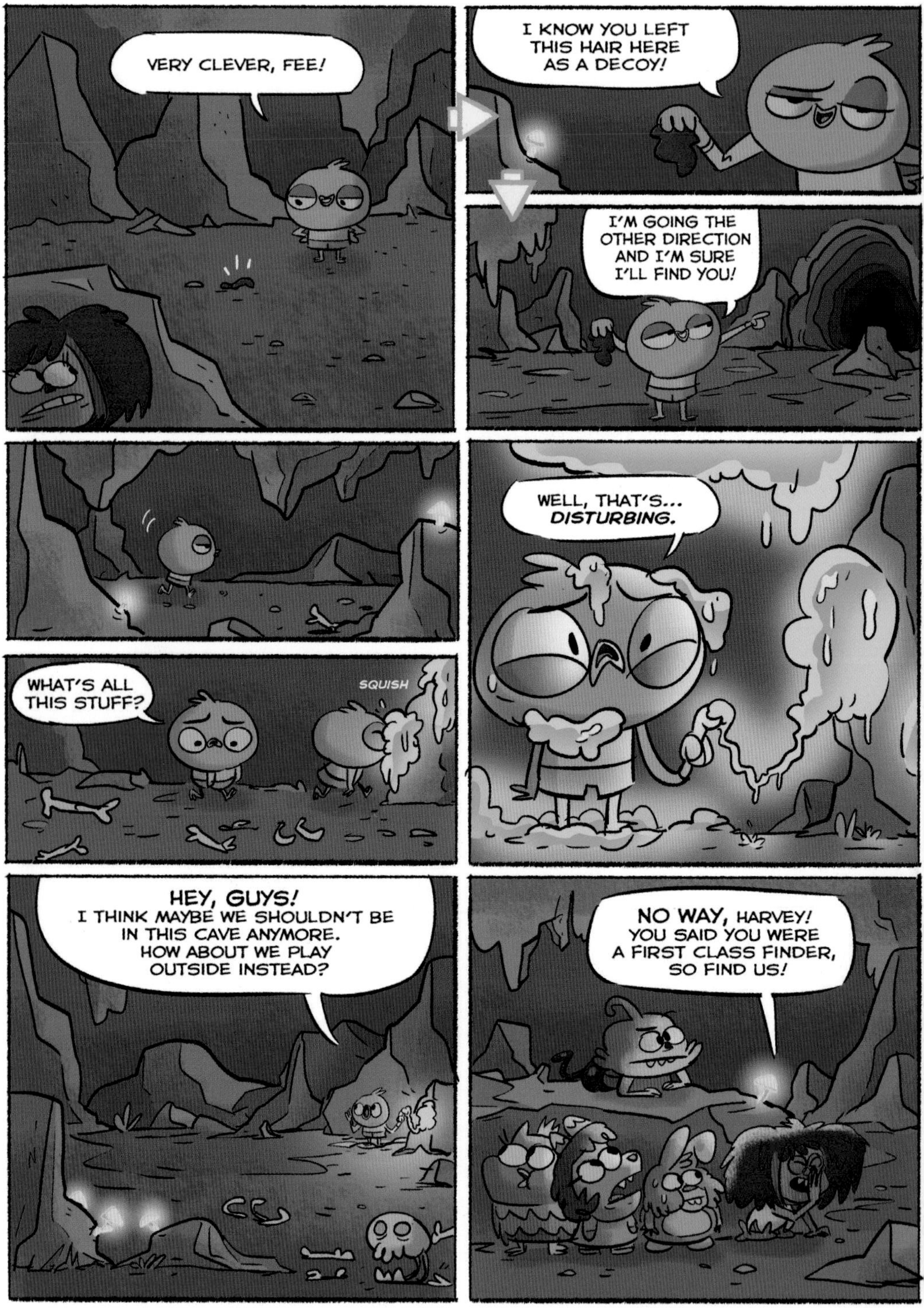
VERY CLEVER, FEE!
I KNOW YOU LEFT THIS HAIR HERE AS A DECOY!
I'M GOING THE OTHER DIRECTION AND I'M SURE I'LL FIND YOU!
WHAT'S ALL THIS STUFF?
SQUISH
WELL, THAT'S... DISTURBING.
HEY, GUYS! I THINK MAYBE WE SHOULDN'T BE IN THIS CAVE ANYMORE. HOW ABOUT WE PLAY OUTSIDE INSTEAD?
NO WAY, HARVEY! YOU SAID YOU WERE A FIRST CLASS FINDER, SO FIND US!

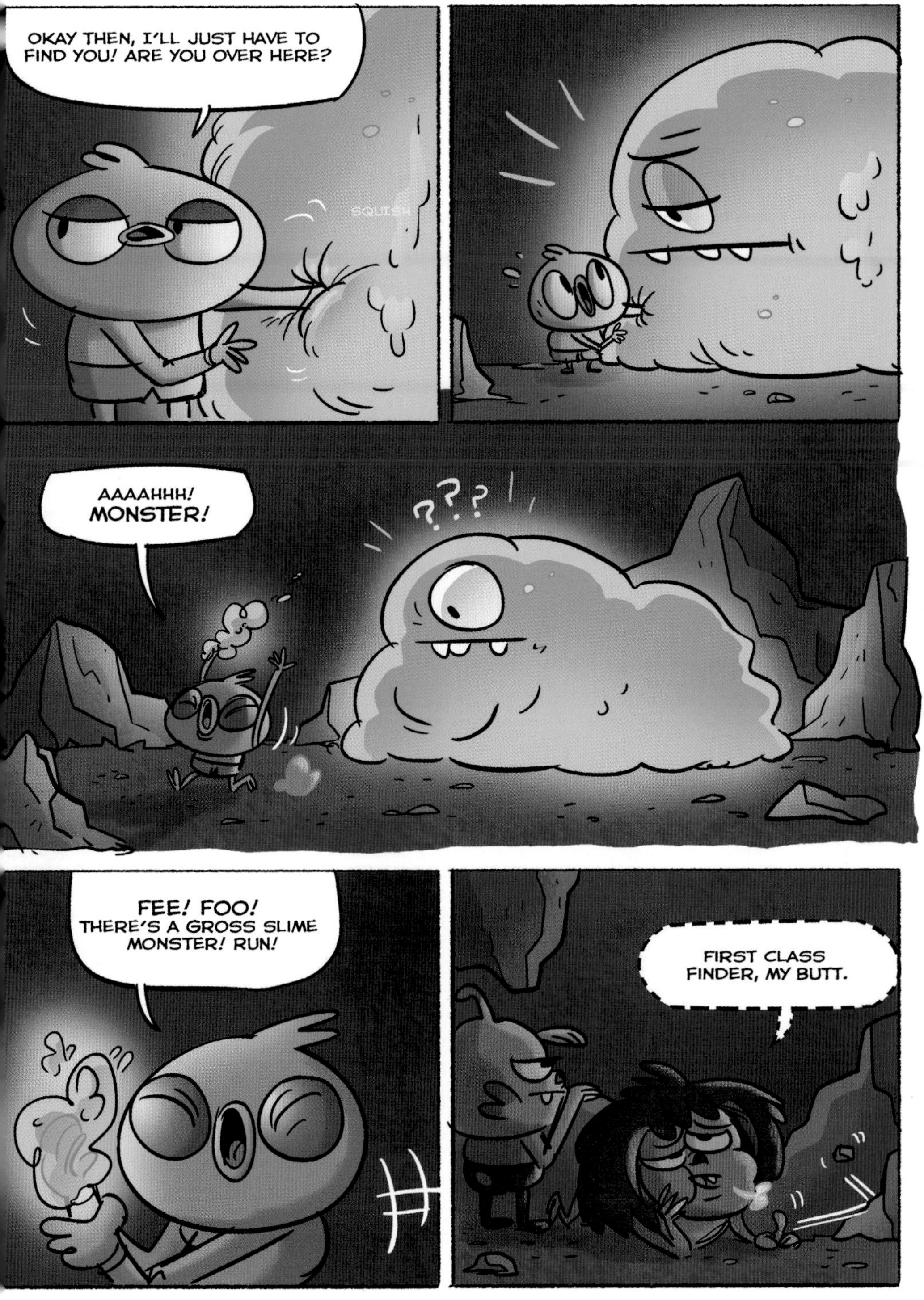
OKAY THEN, I'LL JUST HAVE TO FIND YOU! ARE YOU OVER HERE?
SQUISH
???
AAAAHHH! MONSTER!
FEE! FOO! THERE'S A GROSS SLIME MONSTER! RUN!
FIRST CLASS FINDER, MY BUTT.

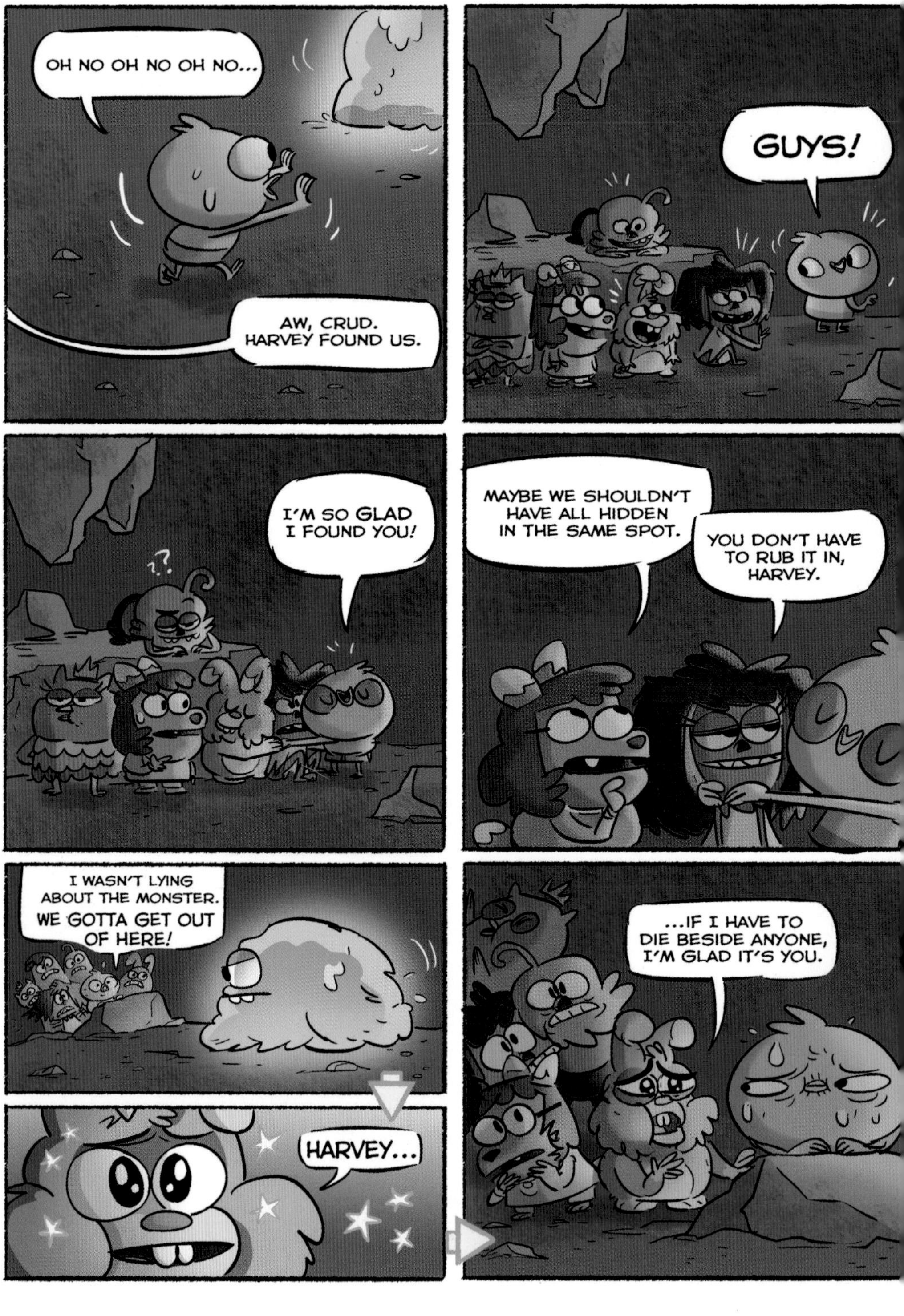
OH NO OH NO OH NO...
AW, CRUD. HARVEY FOUND US.
GUYS!
I'M SO GLAD I FOUND YOU!
MAYBE WE SHOULDN'T HAVE ALL HIDDEN IN THE SAME SPOT.
YOU DON'T HAVE TO RUB IT IN, HARVEY.
I WASN'T LYING ABOUT THE MONSTER. WE GOTTA GET OUT OF HERE!
HARVEY...
...IF I HAVE TO DIE BESIDE ANYONE, I'M GLAD IT'S YOU.

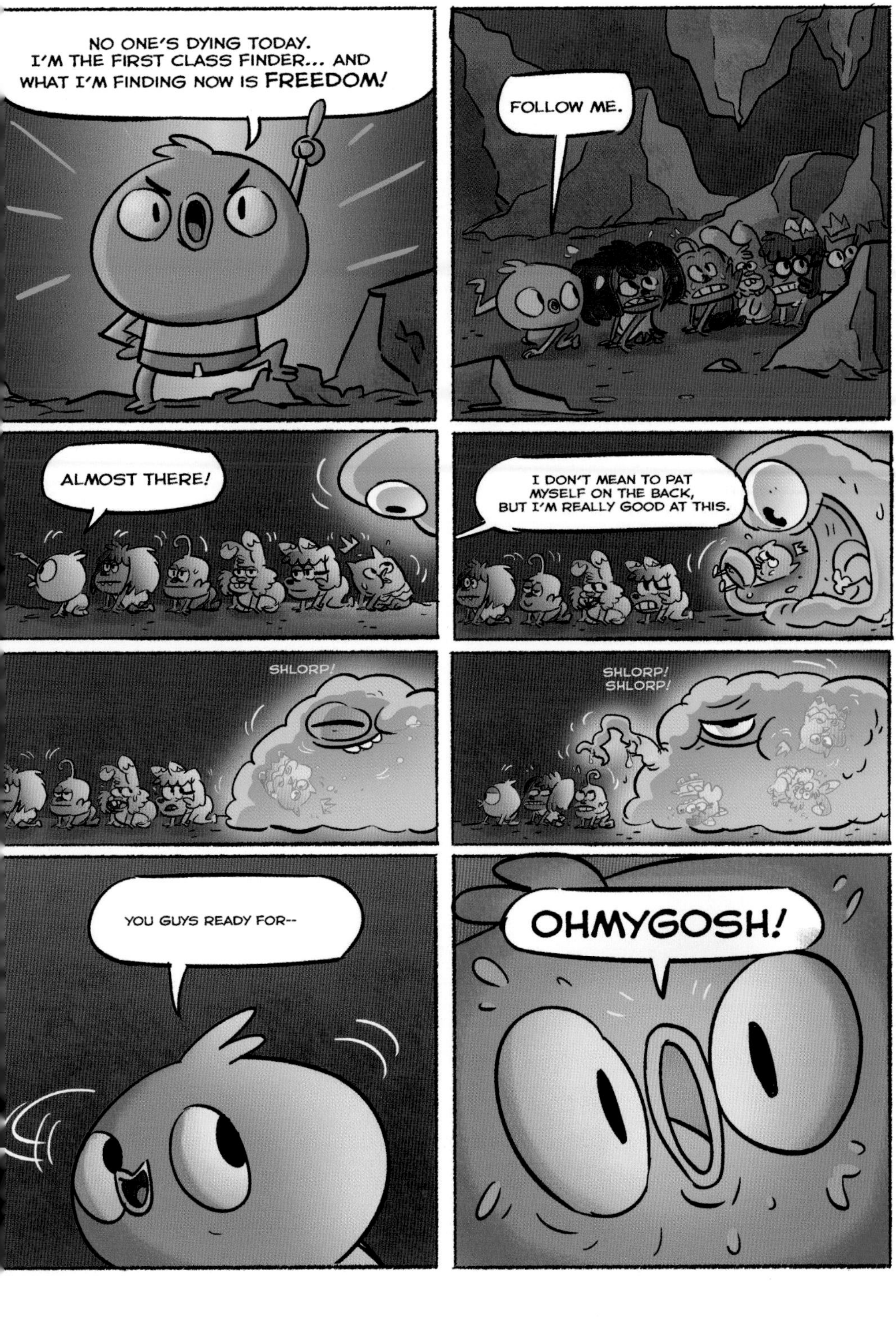
NO ONE'S DYING TODAY. I'M THE FIRST CLASS FINDER... AND WHAT I'M FINDING NOW IS FREEDOM!
FOLLOW ME.
ALMOST THERE!
I DON'T MEAN TO PAT MYSELF ON THE BACK, BUT I'M REALLY GOOD AT THIS.
SHLORP!
SHLORP! SHLORP!
YOU GUYS READY FOR--
OHMYGOSH!

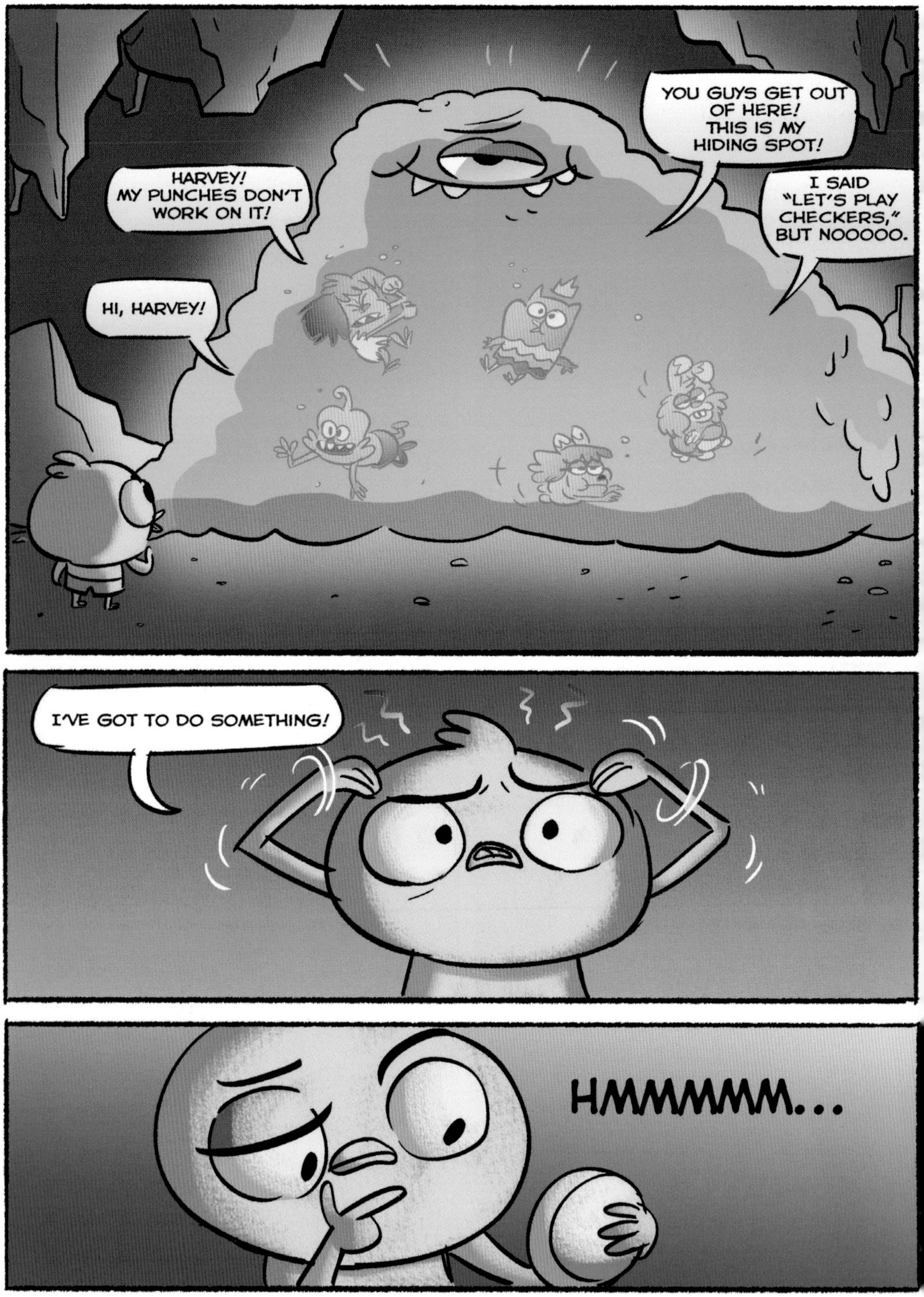
YOU GUYS GET OUT OF HERE! THIS IS MY HIDING SPOT!
HARVEY! MY PUNCHES DON'T WORK ON IT!
I SAID "LET'S PLAY CHECKERS," BUT NOOOOO.
HI, HARVEY!
I'VE GOT TO DO SOMETHING!
HMMMMM...

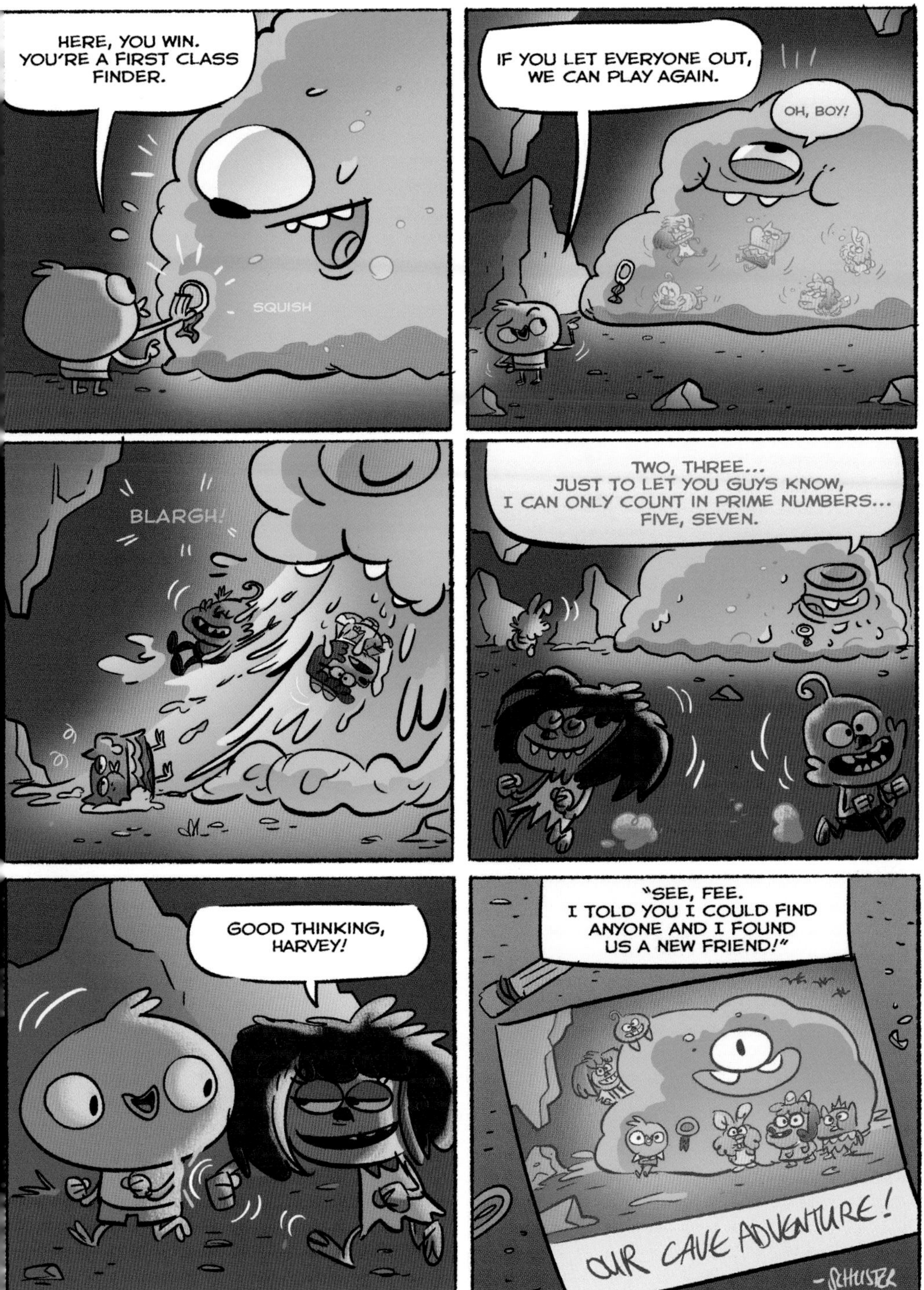
HERE, YOU WIN. YOU'RE A FIRST CLASS FINDER.
SQUISH
IF YOU LET EVERYONE OUT, WE CAN PLAY AGAIN.
OH, BOY!
BLARGH!
TWO, THREE... JUST TO LET YOU GUYS KNOW, I CAN ONLY COUNT IN PRIME NUMBERS... FIVE, SEVEN.
GOOD THINKING, HARVEY!
"SEE, FEE. I TOLD YOU I COULD FIND ANYONE AND I FOUND US A NEW FRIEND!"
OUR CAVE ADVENTURE!
-SCHUSTER

END

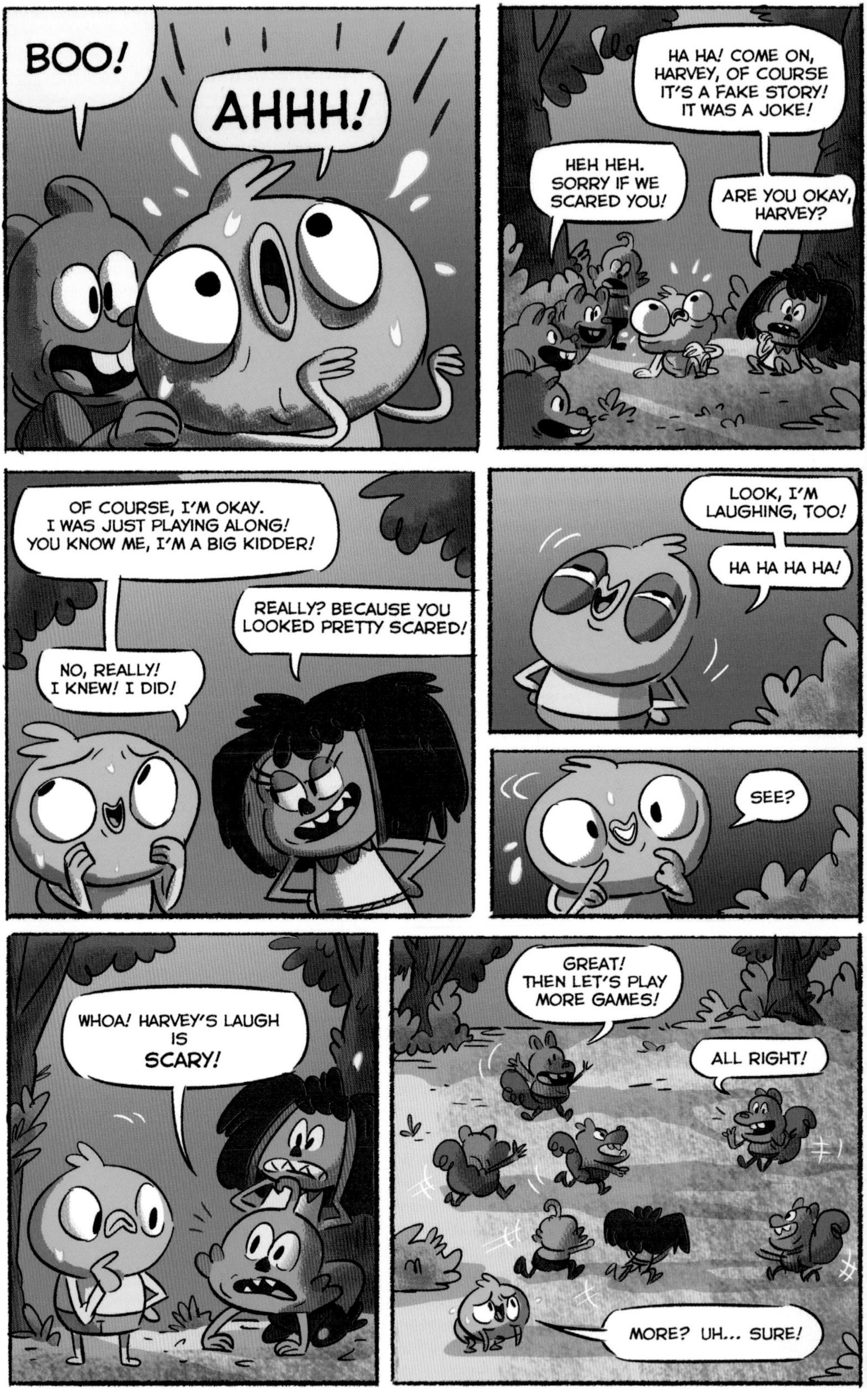
BOO!
AHHH!
HA HA! COME ON, HARVEY, OF COURSE IT'S A FAKE STORY! IT WAS A JOKE!
HEH HEH. SORRY IF WE SCARED YOU!
ARE YOU OKAY, HARVEY?
OF COURSE, I'M OKAY. I WAS JUST PLAYING ALONG! YOU KNOW ME, I'M A BIG KIDDER!
REALLY? BECAUSE YOU LOOKED PRETTY SCARED!
NO, REALLY! I KNEW! I DID!
LOOK, I'M LAUGHING, TOO!
HA HA HA HA!
SEE?
WHOA! HARVEY'S LAUGH IS SCARY!
GREAT! THEN LET'S PLAY MORE GAMES!
ALL RIGHT!
MORE? UH... SURE!

29

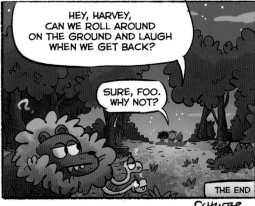

33

SCHUSTER

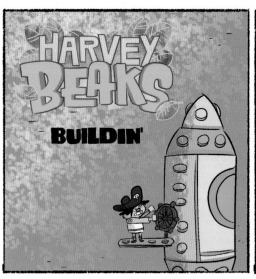

HARVEY BEAKS

BUILDIN'

THE FUSELAGE AND THRUSTERS AREN'T QUITE ON MODEL... BUT SHE SHOULD STILL BE ABLE TO RESCUE PRINCESS MARMAR FROM THE EVIL SPACE BEANS!

BRRRRING!

THIS IS HARVEY SPEAKING.

'SUP, BRO?

OH, TECHNOBEAR!

'SUP, BRO?

H-MAN, LEMME CUT TO DA CHASE.

YOU SEEM LIKE A MAN OF MANY TALENTS. YOU KNOW ANYTHING ABOUT BUILDIN'?

FIRST OFF, WOW. THAT'S REALLY FLATTERING, DUDE. SECONDLY, YEAH! HECK, I'M BUILDIN' AS WE SPEAK!

SWEET! SEE, THERE'S A JUNIOR BUILDIN' COMPETITION TODAY AT THE REC CENTER. BUT IT'S A TEAM THING AND I DON'T HAVE A PARTNER.

35

LATER...

NAME?

HARVEY BEAKS, MA'AM. ALSO, ARE WE ALLOWED TO USE OUR OWN BUILDING MATERIALS OR ARE THEY PROVIDED? I BROUGHT MINE JUST IN CASE.

YEAH, WHATEVER. THIS WAY PLEASE.

WOO! LET THE BUILDING COMMENCE!

MAKE THOSE TRAPS POP, BRO! POP!

≥NGHHH≤

HMM. THESE BUILDERS SURE ARE A LOT MORE MUSCULAR AND NAKED THAN I EXPECTED... BUT, HEY, WHATEVER BUILDS YOUR BOAT, THAT'S WHAT I ALWAYS SAY.

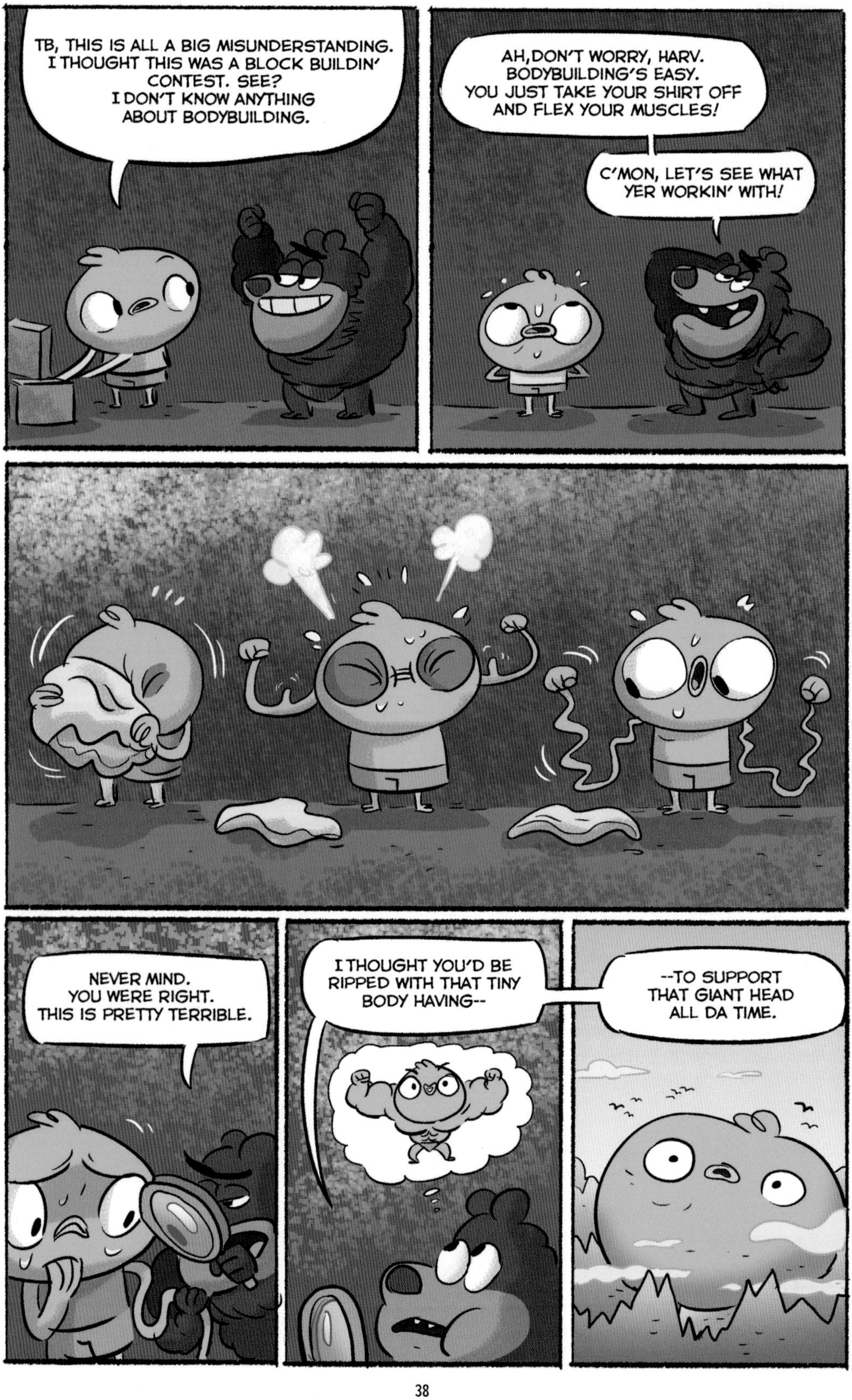

TB, THIS IS ALL A BIG MISUNDERSTANDING. I THOUGHT THIS WAS A BLOCK BUILDIN' CONTEST. SEE? I DON'T KNOW ANYTHING ABOUT BODYBUILDING.
AH, DON'T WORRY, HARV. BODYBUILDING'S EASY. YOU JUST TAKE YOUR SHIRT OFF AND FLEX YOUR MUSCLES!
C'MON, LET'S SEE WHAT YER WORKIN' WITH!
NEVER MIND. YOU WERE RIGHT. THIS IS PRETTY TERRIBLE.
I THOUGHT YOU'D BE RIPPED WITH THAT TINY BODY HAVING--
--TO SUPPORT THAT GIANT HEAD ALL DA TIME.

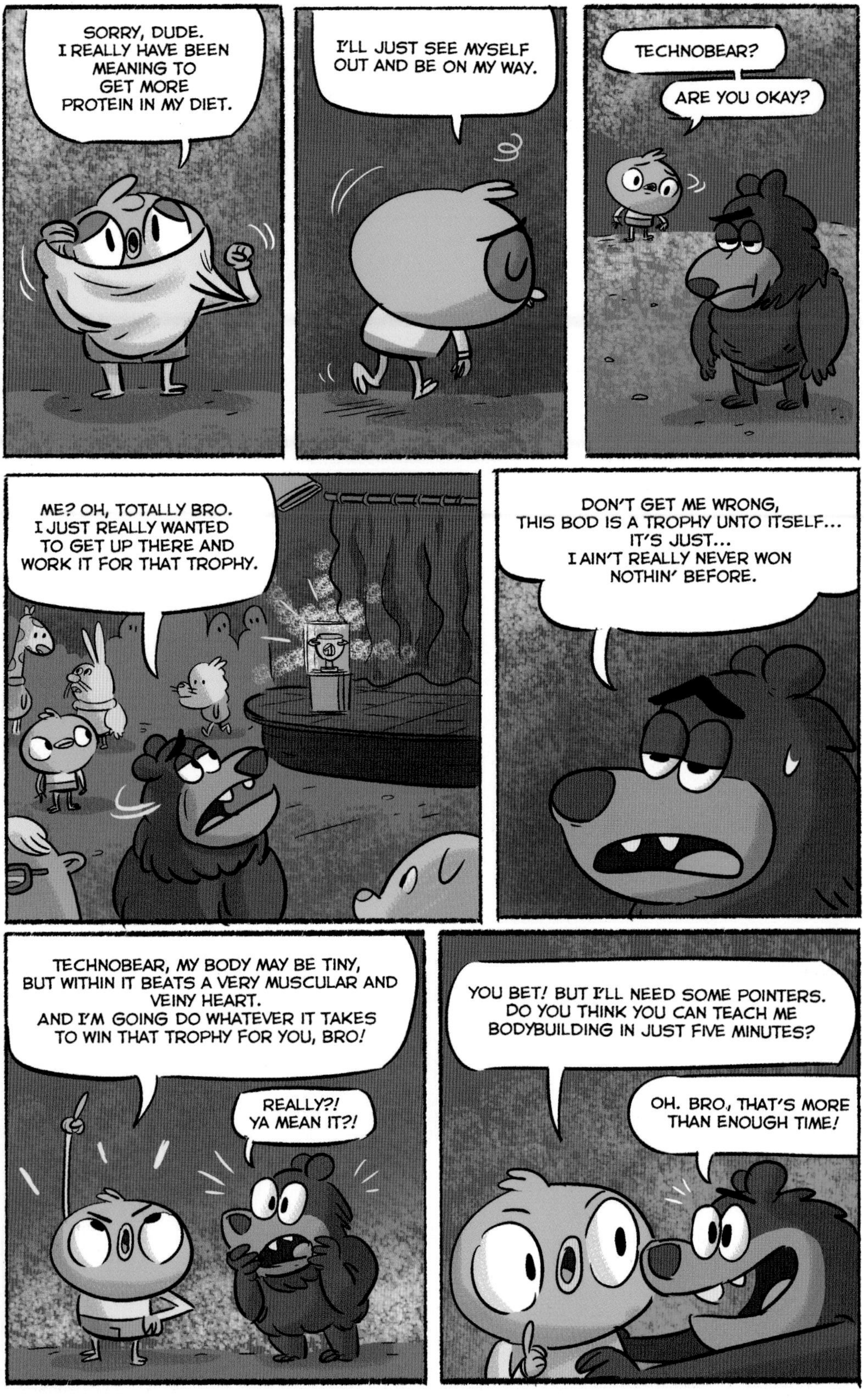
SORRY, DUDE. I REALLY HAVE BEEN MEANING TO GET MORE PROTEIN IN MY DIET.
I'LL JUST SEE MYSELF OUT AND BE ON MY WAY.
TECHNOBEAR?
ARE YOU OKAY?
ME? OH, TOTALLY BRO. I JUST REALLY WANTED TO GET UP THERE AND WORK IT FOR THAT TROPHY.
DON'T GET ME WRONG, THIS BOD IS A TROPHY UNTO ITSELF... IT'S JUST... I AIN'T REALLY NEVER WON NOTHIN' BEFORE.
TECHNOBEAR, MY BODY MAY BE TINY, BUT WITHIN IT BEATS A VERY MUSCULAR AND VEINY HEART. AND I'M GOING DO WHATEVER IT TAKES TO WIN THAT TROPHY FOR YOU, BRO!
REALLY?! YA MEAN IT?!
YOU BET! BUT I'LL NEED SOME POINTERS. DO YOU THINK YOU CAN TEACH ME BODYBUILDING IN JUST FIVE MINUTES?
OH. BRO, THAT'S MORE THAN ENOUGH TIME!

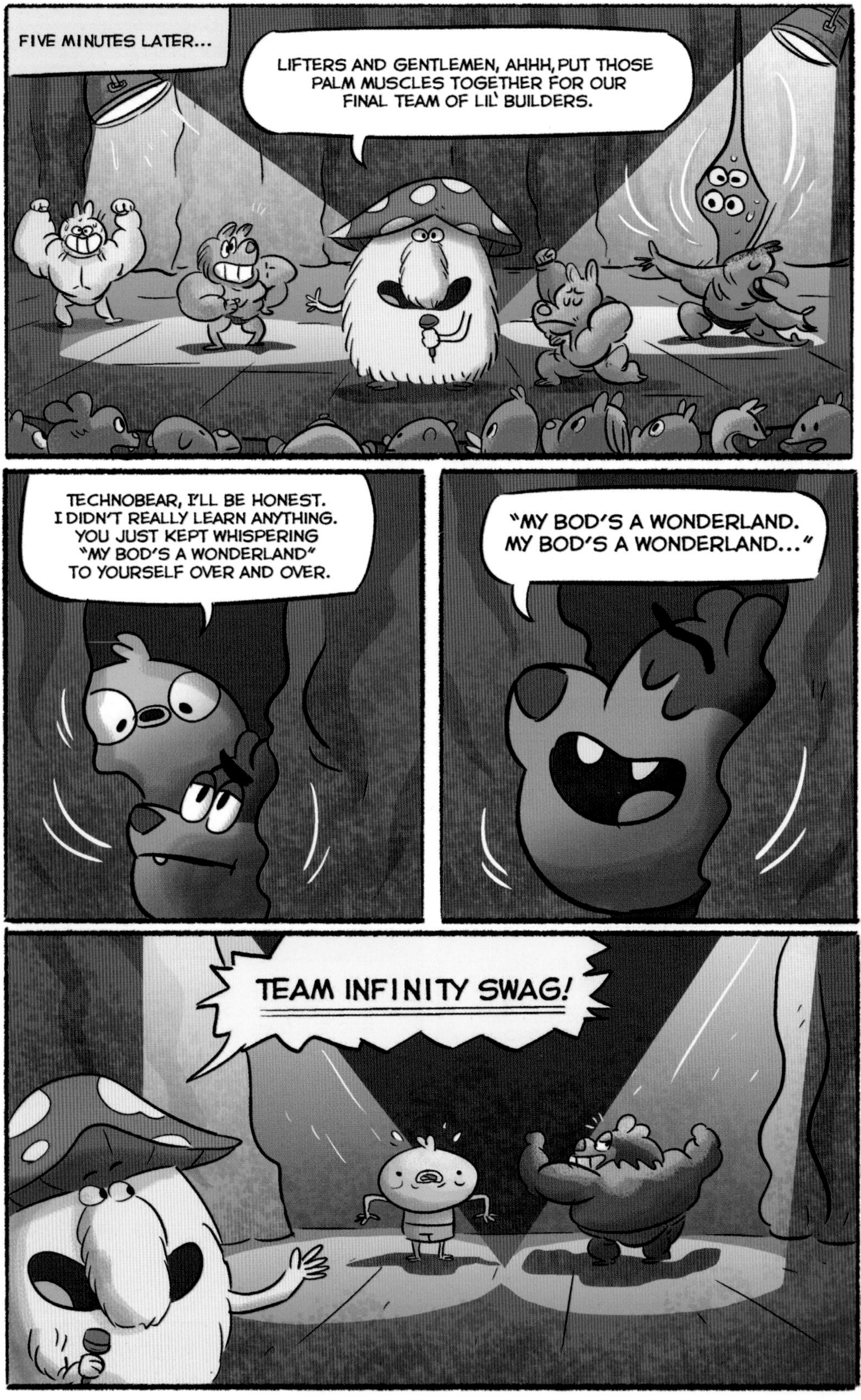
FIVE MINUTES LATER...
LIFTERS AND GENTLEMEN, AHHH, PUT THOSE PALM MUSCLES TOGETHER FOR OUR FINAL TEAM OF LIL' BUILDERS.
TECHNOBEAR, I'LL BE HONEST. I DIDN'T REALLY LEARN ANYTHING. YOU JUST KEPT WHISPERING "MY BOD'S A WONDERLAND" TO YOURSELF OVER AND OVER.
"MY BOD'S A WONDERLAND. MY BOD'S A WONDERLAND..."
TEAM INFINITY SWAG!

41

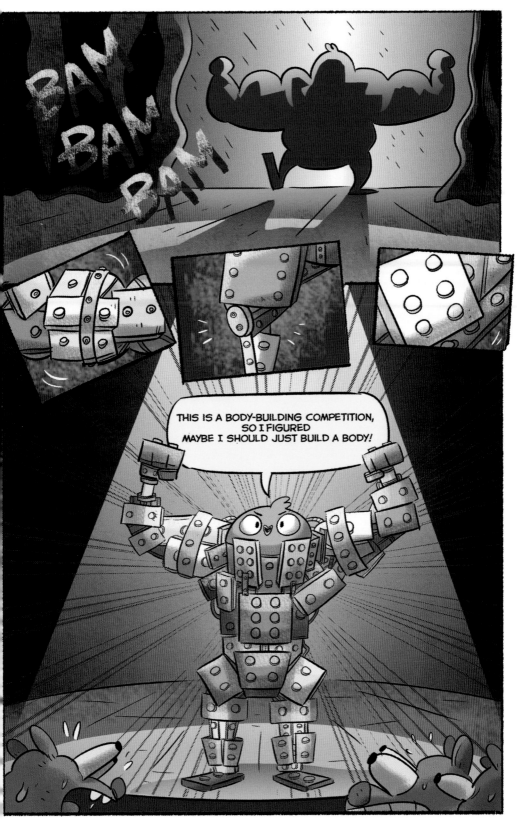

END

WATCH OUT FOR PAPERCUTZ

Welcome to fun-seeking, forest-friendly first HARVEY BEAKS graphic novel from Papercutz—those cuddly critters dedicated to publishing great graphic novels for all ages. I'm Jim Salicrup, the city-dwelling Editor-in-Chief, and I'm here to take you behind-the-scenes at Papercutz...

 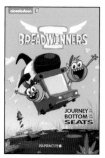

If you've picked up either the SANJAY AND CRAIG or BREADWINNERS graphic novels, you already know most of this. But for those of you just hopping on the Papercutz bandwagon, here's the story of how these graphic novels came to be. A little over ten years ago, Papercutz publisher Terry Nantier and I founded this little comicbook company to address a need—there just didn't seem to be enough comics and graphic novels for kids. That was incredibly ironic, since most folks think of comics as being for kids. After ten years of producing all types of comics for all ages, we made an incredible deal with the awesome folks at Nickelodeon to create a line of graphic novels based on their latest and greatest new animated series. This really is a match made in cartoon heaven -- Nickelodeon, loved my millions of kids for their brilliant cartoon shows and characters, and Papercutz, the graphic novel publisher devoted to creating the best comics for kids—together at last!

Terry and I, along with Joan Hilty and Linda Lee, got to spend a day at the Nickelodeon Animation Studio where we talked about our plans with the creators of Sanjay and Craig, Breadwinners, Harvey Beaks, and more. Everyone was excited and as thrilled as we were about the characters leaping off the TV screen and onto the comicbook page!

To kick off this historic publishing partnership, we launched an all-new NICKELODEON MAGAZINE, which in addition to features such as posters, activities, calendars, etc., is jam-packed with comics—the very same comics we'll be collecting in our graphic novels. The magazine is available wherever magazines are sold, and is also available by subscription. Just go to papercutz.com/nickmag for all the details.

Editors Michael Petranek and Suzannah Rowntree helped get the comics started, but the bulk of the editorial work was handled by Bethany Bryan (Associate Editor/Papercutz) and Joan Hilty (Comics Editor/Nickelodeon). Together, working with writer Stefan Petrucha, Carson Montgomery, Shane Houghton, artist Andreas Schuster, and colorists Laurie E. Smith and Matt Herms, they've come up with the HARVEY BEAKS graphic novel you see before you.

But this is just the beginning! Coming up next will be the debut of the first PIG GOAT BANANA CRICKET graphic novel! Is this the Nickelodeon Age of graphic novels or what? And the best part is that you are a BIG part of it! Tell us what you think of what we're doing—you're opinion matters to us. Our goal is to produce graphic novels that you will love as much as the original TV shows. Write to us at the addresses below and tell us if we succeeded or not. We'll be waiting for your comments!

Thanks,

Jim

STAY IN TOUCH!

EMAIL: salicrup@papercutz.com
WEB: papercutz.com
TWITTER: @papercutzgn
FACEBOOK: PAPERCUTZGRAPHICNOVELS
FANMAIL: Papercutz, 160 Broadway, Suite 700, East Wing, New York, NY 10038

47

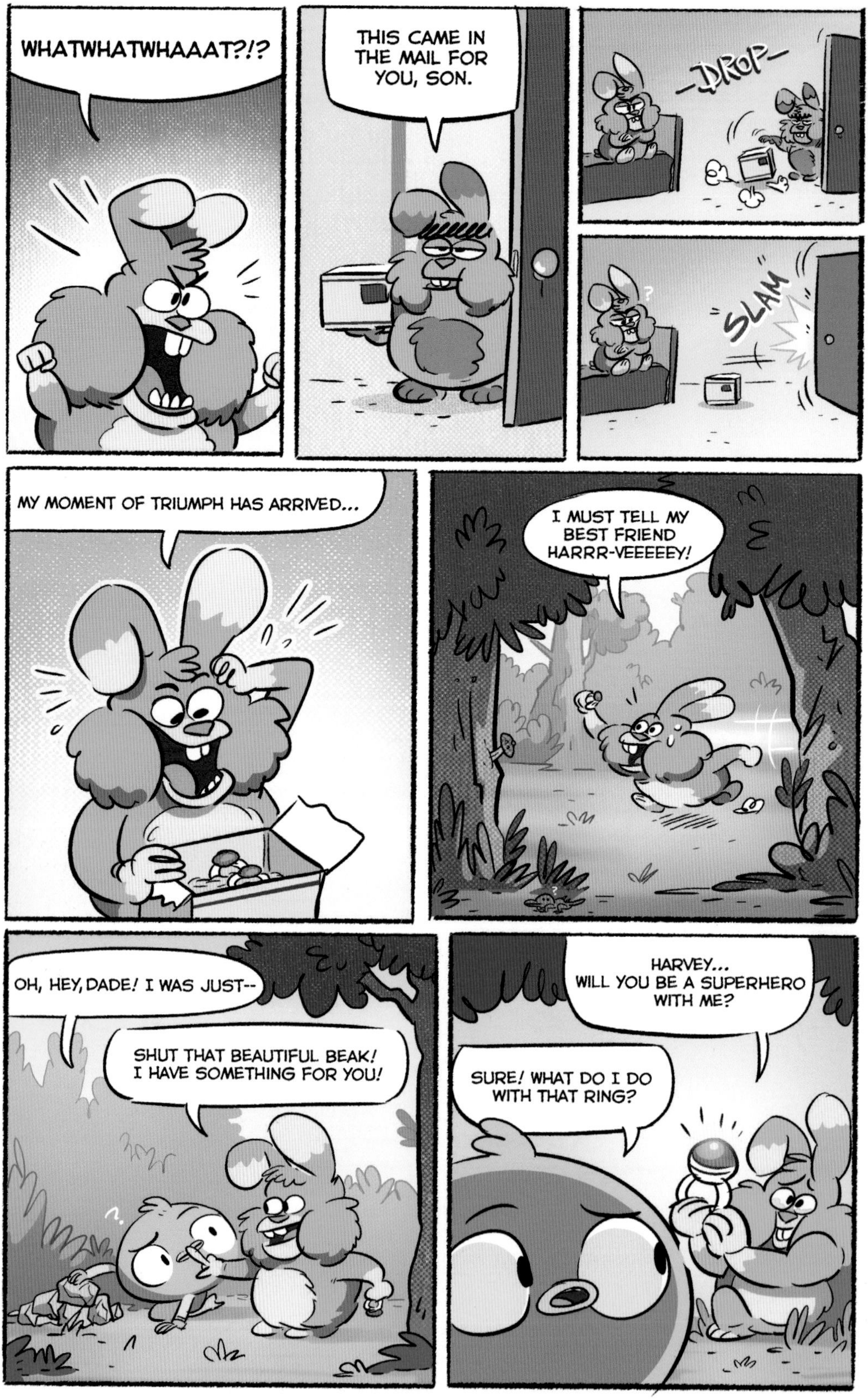

WHATWHATWHAAAT?!?
THIS CAME IN THE MAIL FOR YOU, SON.
-DROP-
SLAM
MY MOMENT OF TRIUMPH HAS ARRIVED...
I MUST TELL MY BEST FRIEND HARRR-VEEEEEY!
OH, HEY, DADE! I WAS JUST--
SHUT THAT BEAUTIFUL BEAK! I HAVE SOMETHING FOR YOU!
HARVEY... WILL YOU BE A SUPERHERO WITH ME?
SURE! WHAT DO I DO WITH THAT RING?

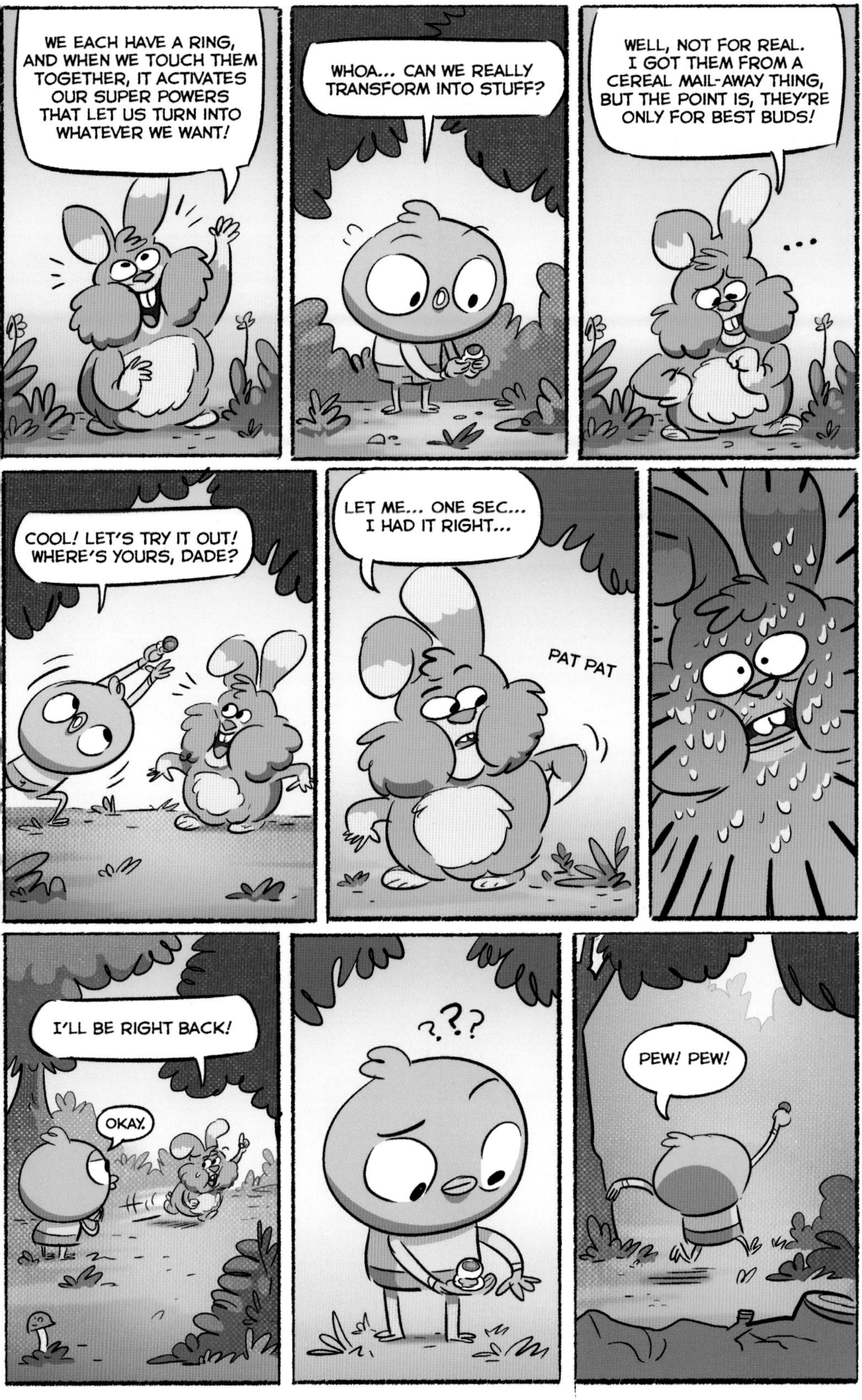
WE EACH HAVE A RING, AND WHEN WE TOUCH THEM TOGETHER, IT ACTIVATES OUR SUPER POWERS THAT LET US TURN INTO WHATEVER WE WANT!
WHOA... CAN WE REALLY TRANSFORM INTO STUFF?
WELL, NOT FOR REAL. I GOT THEM FROM A CEREAL MAIL-AWAY THING, BUT THE POINT IS, THEY'RE ONLY FOR BEST BUDS!
...
COOL! LET'S TRY IT OUT! WHERE'S YOURS, DADE?
LET ME... ONE SEC... I HAD IT RIGHT...
PAT PAT
I'LL BE RIGHT BACK!
OKAY.
?.??
PEW! PEW!

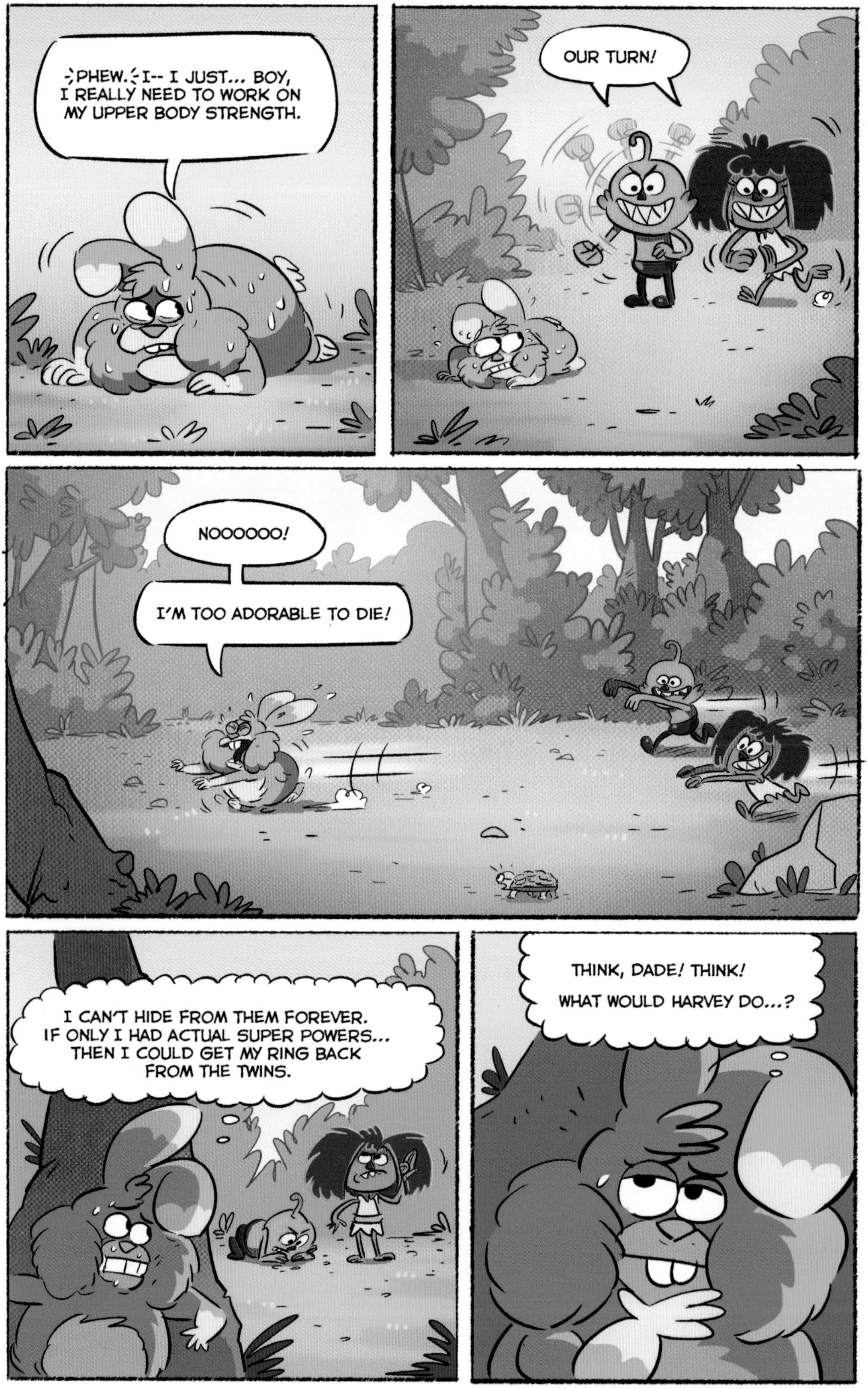
PHEW. I-- I JUST... BOY, I REALLY NEED TO WORK ON MY UPPER BODY STRENGTH.
OUR TURN!
NOOOOOO!
I'M TOO ADORABLE TO DIE!
I CAN'T HIDE FROM THEM FOREVER. IF ONLY I HAD ACTUAL SUPER POWERS... THEN I COULD GET MY RING BACK FROM THE TWINS.
THINK, DADE! THINK!
WHAT WOULD HARVEY DO...?

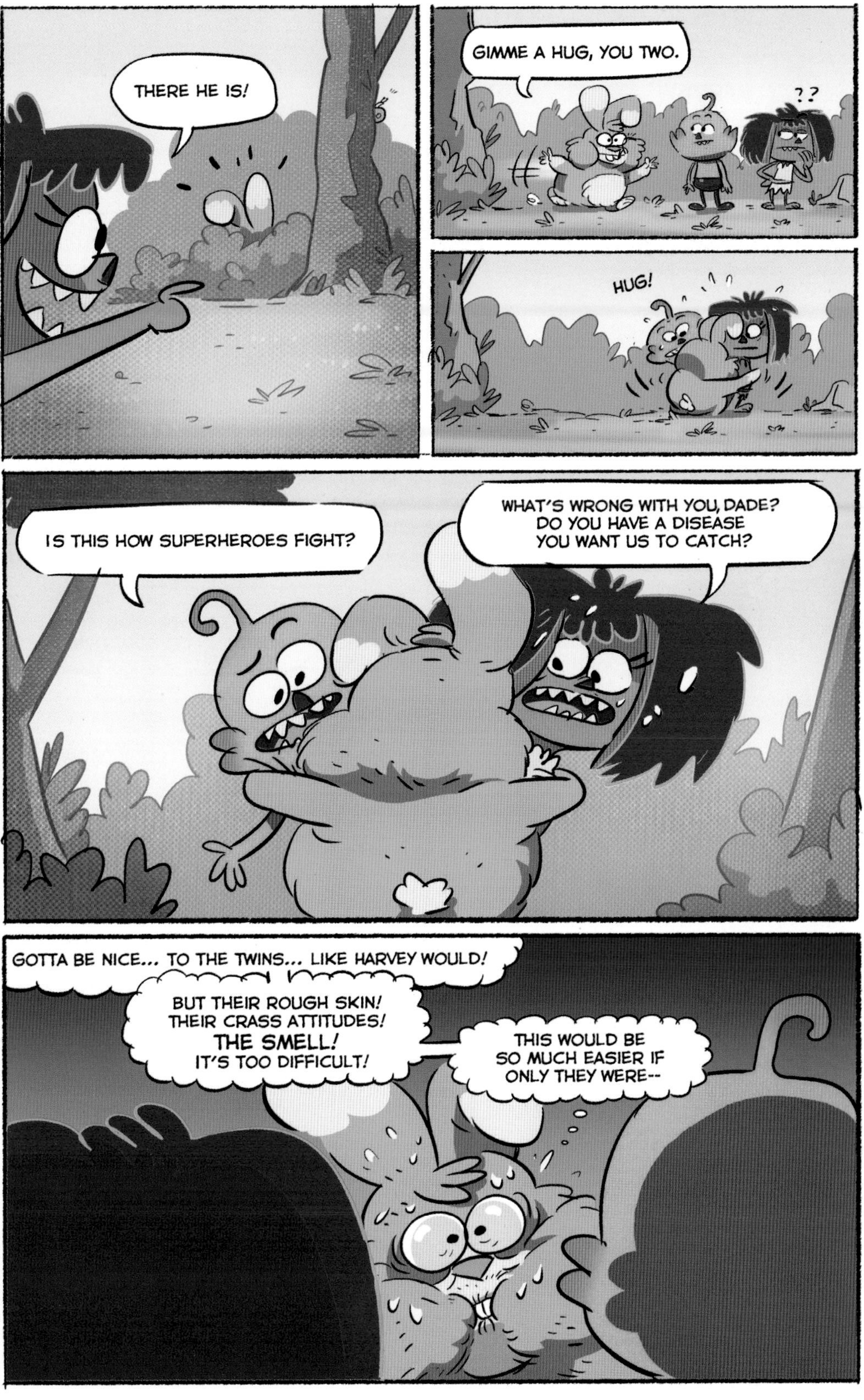
THERE HE IS!
GIMME A HUG, YOU TWO.
??
HUG!
IS THIS HOW SUPERHEROES FIGHT?
WHAT'S WRONG WITH YOU, DADE? DO YOU HAVE A DISEASE YOU WANT US TO CATCH?
GOTTA BE NICE... TO THE TWINS... LIKE HARVEY WOULD!
BUT THEIR ROUGH SKIN! THEIR CRASS ATTITUDES! THE SMELL! IT'S TOO DIFFICULT!
THIS WOULD BE SO MUCH EASIER IF ONLY THEY WERE--

END